PARANORMAL COZY MYSTERY

Scones & Tombstones

TRIXIE SILVERTALE

Sittin' On A Goldmine Productions L.L.C.

Sittin' On A Goldmine Productions, L.L.C.

info@sittinonagoldmine.co

www.sittinonagoldmine.co

ISBN: 978-1-952739-80-4

Cover Design © Sittin' On A Goldmine Productions, L.L.C.

Trixie Silvertale
Scones and Tombstones: Paranormal Cozy Mystery : a novel / by
Trixie Silvertale — 1st ed.

[1. Paranormal Cozy Mystery — Fiction. 2. Cozy Mystery — Fiction. 3. Amateur Sleuths — Fiction. 4. Female Sleuth — Fiction. 5. Wit and Humor — Fiction.] 1. Title.

CHAPTER 1

I'VE NEVER GIVEN MUCH THOUGHT to my bucket list. But now that I've reached the ripe old age of twenty-four, it might be time to start.

Growing up a child of a single parent, we never had extra money. My mother always made sure I had food, school clothes, and a roof over my head. To be honest, I never realized how precious those things were until they were all taken away from me. Losing my wonderful mother when I was only eleven years old changed my life in ways I can barely begin to explain.

Today, I'm going to start taking back some of the things I thought were lost forever—starting with October 31st.

My mother and I loved Halloween! She always made my costumes by hand and took me door-to-door trick-or-treating in our neighborhood. All Hallows' Eve seemed so magical. All I had to do was smile, utter the magic words "trick-or-treat," and a few hours later I marched home with a pillowcase full of candy and a smile from east to west.

The sweets were great, but my favorite part was bedtime. Coraline Moon used to tell me ghost stories as I fell asleep. The belly full of candy, and the resulting sugar high, usually kept me up longer than her. The stories were never too scary—just spooky enough. One of my favorites was a convoluted tale she wove about an enormous haunted house that seemed alive. In the months between magical mischief nights, I would question her ceaselessly about the details of this house.

The way she described it made the tale come to life in my young mind, and I felt certain it really existed somewhere in the world.

Guess what? Now it does!

Using one of my special psychic abilities, I recalled several of these memories from childhood. As I relived her terrific tales, I made meticulous notes. The Duncan-Moon Philanthropic Foundation will host an enormous haunted house this Halloween. All proceeds and donations will be used to fund groundskeeping at the Queen of Heaven Pet Cemetery and to cover operational expenditures at the local no-kill animal shelter.

I chose the gargantuan Barnes estate for the site of my venture. The mansion is available for charitable events due to some unfortunate circumstances in their family, but that's another story.

Cut to—

Parking my Jeep in front of the transformed mansion, I clap my hands together and squeal with delight. Spooky scarecrows line the drive, and they've affixed a tattered wooden gate to the normally imposing iron. A huge sign warning visitors to "Beware" looms overhead.

I step through the gate and gasp. There must be a hundred carved pumpkins edging the path and spilling from the porch. Muslin ghosts float beneath the bare branches of several trees. Motorized bats zip back and forth along monofilament lines, while spooky sounds echo from speakers hidden amongst the décor.

Just when I think I've seen it all, my gaze falls on a face with glowing eyes peering from an upstairs window, and chains rattle from the depths of the home.

I'm blown away, and this is all before I make it through the front door.

As I walk up the steps, the doorman opens the large entrance and I grin. "Hello, Clyde. Everything looks amazing! Did you have anything to do with this?" The gentle giant is a remnant from the home's glory days, and continues to serve as one of two permanent staff at the estate.

He smiles, but embarrassment causes him to stare at the ground.

"It's okay to take credit for doing an amazing job."

He gazes up at me and his large, soft eyes spill over with gratitude. "Thank you, Miss Moon. I like helping."

Before I can coerce him to elaborate on what he specifically enjoyed, his mother, Mrs. Charles, the caretaker of the charitable estate, appears from nowhere and ushers me inside. "Good day, Miss Moon. I hope the preparations meet with your satis-faction."

"It's stunning so far. What else do you have to show me?"

"This way, please. As you know, the upper floors of the manor will be off limits to guests, but I'll guide you around the ground floor. They have designed each room as a separate experience."

The hall of portraits, as the first room is called, houses various spooky paintings with eyes that follow you across the room. Plus, some of the im-ages transform into vaporous holographic ghosts that float through the air overhead. Clearly no ex-pense has been spared on special effects.

We travel into the next room where the door

slams behind us and the candles snuff out. Eerie cackling echoes from the corners, and a hidden door in the far wall slides open.

As we slip into the next experience, I hear whispering voices and feel something brush against my back.

"Wow! This is exactly what I wanted. It's totally scary, but not gory. I want people to feel a little fright, not be sick to their stomach."

She hastily nods her agreement. "Indeed. There were a couple of installations that I insisted they remove. I would not have a questionable butcher's shop, or any hint of torture."

"Good call. I don't want that either. I want this to be an attraction that families feel comfortable bringing their children to."

She nodded firmly. "I agree wholeheartedly, Miss Moon."

"I'd love to see the graveyard. Is it finished?"

A perfunctory smile indicates that I'm foolish in questioning her efficiency. "Follow me." She leads the way out the French doors to the garden patio and down the large granite steps. Thick fog rolls across the ground, and the haunting call of graveyard ghosts echoes through the tombstones.

"This is fantastic!" I walk among the headstones and give a genuine scream when one coffin bursts to the surface and pops open to reveal a plastic skeleton.

She hurries to my side. "Is it too much? I shall have it removed at once if you feel it's unnecessary."

"It's all perfect! It's exactly as my mother described."

"Begging your pardon, Miss. I didn't quite catch that. I'm a tad hard of hearing." Mrs. Charles cups her hands behind her left ear and leans toward me. "Suffered some hearing loss from a factory job I had in my youth."

"Oh, it was nothing important. I was only commenting on how wonderfully everything is coming together. It's absolutely perfect."

She smiles, but the expression does not touch her eyes. It's as though she expects nothing less of herself.

"However, I'm afraid I have to ask about the safety requirements that Sheriff Harper placed on our permit. Do we have the required number of emergency exits? And a clear evacuation plan in case of fire?"

She reaches into the pocket of her utilitarian black dress and extracts a folded paper. "These are the emergency exits. There are also panic buttons at three separate locations should a patron want to leave the experience for any reason. The dashed green line represents the various evacuation routes in case of fire—or some other unforeseen mal-function."

"Flawless. If I can get a copy of that to pass along—"

"I messengered a copy to Sheriff Harper this morning."

"Wonderful. I look forward to the 'soft' opening. We have buses scheduled to bring the patrons from the book signing directly to this attraction. Our ticket price included the suggested donation for the haunted house. How are you doing with staffing?"

For once, she doesn't have a ready answer. "I'm short a ticket taker. I still have a few days to locate the appropriate personnel, but if you have someone in mind—"

"Did you add the Angel of Death to your count?"

Mrs. Charles clutches her chest in fright. "I beg your pardon?"

"Sorry! I didn't mean to frighten you. I hired a girl to dress as the Angel of Death and check names off the list at the entrance. I was wondering if you remembered to include her?"

"I hadn't. Thank you for reminding me." She nods solemnly. "Much appreciated, Miss Moon."

As I turn to leave, she strides into a small garden shed that must contain the controls for the pop-up cemetery. The fog vanishes and the spooky sensations recede.

During the drive into town, I run through a list of possible Halloween helpers. I may be able to convince my volunteer employee, Twiggy, to moonlight at the haunted house, but seeing to her payment could present a problem. She refuses to take any money for her services at my bookshop, but that's simply because she prefers to be paid in firsthand access to the clumsy shenanigans that make up my daily life.

Stellen would be great at this gig. Unfortunately, my stepbrother and his on-again, off-again girlfriend are both away at school.

Seems like Mrs. Charles has things under control. Plus, Erick and I will be on hand to play our parts and help, if needed.

Mmmmm. Erick. Now there's something yummy to focus on while I drive. It couldn't possibly hurt to stop by the station in person. If I add a little wiggle and wink to my request, it's bound to be more successful.

And just to seal the deal, I'll stop by the patisserie and pick up some flaky, sugary decadence to further stack the deck in my favor.

CHAPTER 2

No sooner have I parked my car on Third Avenue than the luscious aromas wafting from Bless Choux consume me. The lovely scents put the spurs to my giddy-up, and I hurry into the patisserie.

The owner, Anne, flits around behind the counter with a huge smile on her face. I step into the queue, smile, and wave.

For the first time since I discovered this lovely bakery, her eyes lock on me, and her ready smile fades.

Uh oh! What have I done to upset the best baker in almost-Canada? Time seems to stand still as I wait impatiently. Finally reaching the counter, Anne refuses to meet my gaze. "Anne, what's wrong? Did I do something to offend you?"

She shakes her head and sighs. "It's not your fault, Mitzy. I'm sure your heart was in the right place. And I'm more than certain Chiffon Cheryl didn't give you a choice."

Oh dear. When Twiggy accepted the publicist's request for a cookbook launch party at my bookshop, it never occurred to me it might offend my local bakery. "I'm so sorry. It's just a book launch party. If you want, I'll hire you to cater the event. I'm certain your baked goods are twice as good as anything in her recipe book."

Anne sighs and rolls her eyes. "Is this for here or to-go?"

"I'll have a chocolate croissant and a dozen of whatever you want to give me to-go. But I'll have the croissant here if it gives you time to explain."

She nods and inhales sharply. "Thank you. Meet me at the corner table."

I overpay, leave a generous tip, and move my ample backside to the chair in the corner.

As I wait for Anne to join me, I feel a little like a toddler on timeout.

Finally, she heads my way with a pink box and a small plate bearing my chocolate croissant.

"I'm sorry to act like a spoiled child, Mitzy. But Cheryl, or Chiffon Cheryl as she's come to be known, and I were in the CIA together."

I choke on my flaky croissant, and pound my

hand on my chest as I lean forward. "You're a spy? I mean, an agent?"

At last, Anne's ready smile and lighthearted laughter return. "I always forget that has a double meaning. The CIA is the Culinary Institute of America. Cheryl and I were classmates. She seemed like a kind, generous baker, but it was all an act. She used her beguiling ways to get people to let their guard down, and then she stole recipes and sabotaged students to claw her way to the top of the class. In the end, she used her ill-gotten fame to launch an equally fraudulent career. Most of the recipes in her cookbook aren't even her own. Several of them were stolen directly from me! Including my award-winning scones!"

"Dagnabbit! I wish I'd known. I never would've agreed to help her promote that trash. It's not too late for me to cancel the whole thing."

The big-hearted baker reaches across the table and squeezes my hand. "It's incredibly sweet of you to offer, but if you don't host the event, she'll just take it somewhere else. Pin Cherry can always use the publicity. At least you know the truth now." Her shoulders visibly relax.

We share a laugh, and my natural snoopiness kicks in. "I have to ask, why 'Chiffon?' Did she always wear frilly dresses to baking class?"

Anne chuckles. "You sounded like Isadora for a minute there."

My heart warms, and I pretend I don't know all about Myrtle Isadora's fashion obsession. "That's sweet of you to say. I'm sure she was a wonderful woman."

"Oh, she was, but let me tell you the chiffon story. It's not the fabric. In baking class, the chiffon cake was our first test. The key to a winning cake is beating loads of air into the batter and fully incorporating the oil, so you have a fluffy AND moist cake. It's incredibly technical. The instructor chose it as a way to weed out the wheat from the chaff."

As you know, patience isn't my thing, so I blurt, "And Cheryl made the best cake!"

Anne shakes her head. "Not even close. Cheryl recognized talent when she saw it. There was a quiet, shy girl named Maisy who could bake circles around all of us, but she had no confidence. Cheryl pretended to befriend her. On test day, just as her cake was about to pop out of the oven, nerves got the best of Maisy and she needed to run to the ladies' to throw up."

"Yeesh!"

She nods and continues. "Cheryl comforted her and said, 'You go ahead. I'll grab your cake when the timer goes off and set it upside down to cool.'" Anne holds up a finger to derail my interruption.

"The cake has to cool inverted to protect the fluffiness. Anyway, Maisy ran to the bathroom and two oven timers went off almost simultaneously. Cheryl deftly popped her cake out and carried it to Maisy's station to grab the second cake. Then, with a magician's sleight of hand, she swapped the cakes and put Maisy's utterly perfect chiffon cake on her own bench."

"That conniving snake in the grass!"

"Exactly. Well, as you might've predicted. Maisy's cake—which was actually Cheryl's—failed spectacularly, and Maisy was so mortified she dropped out of the CIA. Meanwhile, Cheryl had the best chiffon cake in the class and accepted all the accolades without batting her false eyelashes. At the end of the day, all the students were sampling 'her' cake and saying, 'Amazing chiffon, Cheryl. Great chiffon, Cheryl. You baked a perfect chiffon, Cheryl . . .' and the name kinda stuck."

"Wow! What a terrible tale. I definitely won't be offering to buy any of her books to stock at my shop! But my offer to hire you as caterer stands."

Anne waves my comment away. "I have no interest in stirring up trouble. If it's all the same to you, I'll keep my distance from the whole thing. The last thing I want to do is run into Chiffon Cheryl and say something I'll regret."

As though the mere repetition of her name

could summon her from the ether, the front door of the bakery opens, and Anne's sweet, hopeful face falls like a bad soufflé.

There's no need for me to turn around and verify what my eyes and my extra senses are already telling me.

Chiffon Cheryl has just entered Bless Choux.

This promises to be worse than any unpleasant scene from *Romy and Michele's High School Reunion.*

Cheryl throws her arms in the air and runs across the patisserie on her tiptoes like Edith Bunker from *All in the Family.*

Anne barely has time to rise from her chair before Chiffon Cheryl catches her shoulders and tosses a fake kiss to either side of her astonished face.

"Annie! I just knew you would have a nice little bakery. Oh, Annie. You always were such a clever girl."

Before my chocolate croissant makes an unnecessary reappearance, I hop to my feet and insert myself as a shield between Cheryl and Anne. Thrusting my hand forward, to propel Cheryl back a step or two, I introduce myself. "You must be Chiffon Cheryl! I'm Mitzy Moon, owner of the bookshop where your publicist has arranged the launch party." I'm careful to word my introduction in a way that indicates I didn't go seeking the event, nor was I endorsing it in any way. Which was all true. I hadn't actually charged them for the venue, but her publicist had arranged everything. I mean, maybe Twiggy got some chairs, but that didn't cost us anything. She can call in favors from the bingo hall whenever she needs.

My appearance certainly puts the brakes on Cheryl's wicked plan. She stumbles backward and her bright pink lips work wordlessly like a fish out of water.

Once more unto the breach. "And don't sell Anne short. This is no mere bakery. This is a European-level patisserie. It's been written up in all the foodie magazines." I have no idea whether or not that's true. But guess what? Neither does Cheryl.

Before I can drive the barb any deeper, a mousy woman steps forward to meet my advance. I hadn't even noticed her. She's wrapped in several shades of bland, with a rust-colored fashion scarf tied around her neck. The elaborate knot must be something she learned from an online influencer. It's at odds with her otherwise understated vibe. Thick glasses rest heavily on her sharp nose, and a plain barrette clasps her nondescript hair. Her thin lips attempt a smile, but fail miserably. "I'm Janet Ferro, Cheryl's publicist. We spoke on the phone."

If Janet thinks she can unhorse me so easily, she's sadly mistaken. "Oh, I don't think so. I have someone who handles all of that at the bookshop. You probably spoke to Twiggy. I hardly have time to take phone calls when I'm hanging out at this exquisite patisserie, eating chocolate croissants all day long!" All right, I've had my fun. Now I'm starting to nauseate myself. Without needing Anne's permission, I'm certain she'll appreciate it if I take the trash out with me.

Grabbing my lovely pink pastry box off the table, I turn to the pair and gesture toward the exit. "Why don't you two come back to the bookshop with me? It's only a block or two away, and I'd love for you to take a look at everything Twiggy set up. There's still time to make changes before tomorrow night."

Once again, it pleases me that Cheryl is at a loss for words.

Janet avoids eye contact and mumbles something under her breath, but neither woman resists my directions.

Once we return to the crisp air on Third Avenue, Janet motions toward a waiting car and says something about meeting me at the Bell, Book & Candle.

Fine by me. I don't plan on walking in this brisk wind, anyway. The great lake nestled in our harbor chose today to swirl up a frosty north-easterly tempest. I'm happy to jump back in my Jeep and make a quick stop at the sheriff's station. After all, I have big plans for bribery, and I'm not about to let these tasty treats go to waste.

Twiggy can handle the riffraff if they manage to find their way to the bookstore before me.

CHAPTER 3

AFTER THEY PULL AWAY, I meander toward Main Street and park opposite Myrtle's Diner. This way, I'll have an excuse to poke my head in the door and offer my grandfather a wave before I genuinely jump into my workday.

The swirling wind whips my hair into a frenzy, wraps my soft, striped scarf over my face, and blasts my unzipped jacket nearly off my shoulders. I'm lucky to make it into the sheriff's station with the pastry box intact.

The deputy behind the counter is hard at work playing her favorite game, Furious Monkeys, and even though we have developed great nonverbal communication to accommodate my many visits to the station, I approach the desk and smile. "Good morning, Baird. What level are you?"

She must smell the pastries because she makes highly unusual eye contact, smiles, and pauses her game. "Oh, hiya, Mitzy. I just made it to level 412 this morning. Every time they issue an update, this game gets better and better. What's in the box?" Her eyes linger longingly on the pink cardboard.

"Would you like first pick?" I open the lid, and she smiles gratefully.

"You're a lifesaver. I overslept this morning and ran out of the house without so much as a piece of toast. I thought I'd never make it to lunch. Gosh, I'd love to take that bear claw, but I know those are Paulsen's favorite. I'll settle for the apple fritter."

She takes her pick, and I push through the crooked wooden gate and into the bullpen. It's definitely a slow day, or perhaps the weather is keeping everyone inside. Deputies Paulsen, Johnson, and Gilbert are all seated at their dilapidated metal desks pretending to work on reports—or some such nonsense.

I head straight to Paulsen's desk and open the box. "Morning. Would you like the bear claw?"

Her right hand immediately flinches toward her gun, but when she looks up, there's an odd smile on her face. This may be the first time in memory that she hasn't sneered or snarled in my general direction. "Looks good." She takes the pastry, nods, and returns to her imaginary work.

There was no "thank you," but I'll consider a smile progress. Maybe our shared canoeing adventure has softened a bit of her resentment. But I'm not one to count my chickens before the eggs hatch.

Johnson and Gilbert grab two each, and my pastry box is looking pretty sparse by the time I make it to Erick's office. I'm going to have to pull out all the stops to get what I want.

I halt in the doorway, lean against the doorjamb, and kick out one hip.

It only takes a moment for Erick to peel his eyes from the report in his hands and slowly trace my curves as he works his way up to meet my gaze. "A serving of Mitzy with a side of pastry? This must be my lucky day."

His loving gaze and teasing words bring a flush to my cheeks. Before I can place said pastry box on his desk, he's on his feet and scooping his arms around my waist.

All my rules about public displays of affection have long since been thrown to the wolves. I love him. He loves me. And we don't care who knows about it.

His tender kiss lingers on my lips, and I'm pretty sure I have him exactly where I want him.

Unfortunately, he's onto me. "Hold on. This is no accidental drop-by. I know that look, Moon. Who died?"

Oops. There I go, getting lost in my mind movies and losing my advantage. "Died! No one. Why is it every time I come in here—"

"Oh, don't play innocent with me." A crooked grin lifts the corner of his inviting mouth. "You and I both know you're more of a corpse magnet than a mortuary."

That one brings a hearty chuckle from both of us. "All right, Sheriff Harper. You got me." I put both of my hands in the air as though it's a Wild West stickup. "I was hoping you'd agree to come to the soft opening of my haunted house attraction."

"One question. Am I coming as your boyfriend, or as free security in the form of Pin Cherry Harbor's local sheriff?"

"Erick! I would never abuse our relationship. I'm asking you as my boyfriend. And as the second half of my couples' costume."

Stepping back, he takes a seat on the edge of his well-worn desk. "Do I have to be the back of a horse or something?"

He should know better than giving me a visual like that. Laughter hits me so hard I have to lean over and support myself by placing a hand on my thigh. So many images. Too many movie references. I can barely catch my breath. "Holy stand-up comic. You should take that act on the road, Sheriff."

He crosses his arms in that yummy way that makes his biceps bulge, and my eyes and my tingly tummy are momentarily distracted

"*Ahem.* I have a whole county to look after, Moon. What's the costume?"

"Well, to be honest, I'm kind of sticking it to Grams by going as a zombie bride. I was sort of hoping you'd be my zombie groom."

His eyes widen and his pupils dilate.

It takes every ounce of self-control I don't possess to subdue my psychic senses. Something in my request sparks nervousness or excitement. Oh boy. My snoopy insides are dying to dig into this.

"Look, Moon, if this is your way of steering me out of imagining our future together, I got news for you. You're all out of aces."

"Touché." He has a point. We pretty much placed all our cards on the table when he got back from FBI sleep-away camp. "Not at all. But ever since we had our 'kiss and makeup,' Grams has been hounding me nonstop about when she gets to plan the wedding. So, I pretended I didn't notice she was watching me when I ordered the wedding dress. It's really just a huge Halloween prank to play on a ghost. Can I count you in?"

He rubs a hand over his face as he shakes his head. "I can't believe any of what I'm hearing, and I believe what I'm going to say even less. But, yes. I will help you prank a ghost, Mitzy Moon."

I clap my hands together and jump up and down. "Thank you. Honestly, I owe you big time, Sheriff."

Faster than a rattlesnake striking a pack rat, he loops his arm around my waist and pulls me close. "Careful. I may call that marker due sooner than you think."

And, I'm dead. My knees are jelly, my heart is nearly beating out of my chest, and the only thing I can think of in the entire world is how much I want to kiss his full, pouty mouth.

"Oh, for crying out loud, Sheriff." Paulsen exhales in disgust. "We got a call. Can you two wrap this up?" Without waiting for a reply, stout and round Deputy Paulsen turns on her heels and hastily waddles back to her desk, leaving the soundtrack of polyester rubbing against itself in her wake.

"Well, duty calls, Moon."

Erick disentangles himself and heads for the door of his office.

"Hold on, Sheriff. You didn't answer my question."

He pauses in the doorway and turns his head. His big blue eyes make their best attempt at innocence. "Didn't I?"

"No, you didn't. Are you going to be my zombie groom or not?"

"Oh, of course. I thought I made that clear."

My cheeks flush as I mumble, "Um, you got me all distracted with your wandering hands and your kissable mouth. I don't exactly remember what you said."

He chuckles with self-satisfaction and hustles to catch up with Deputy Paulsen. As they push through the wooden gate, I hear her mention a disturbance at the Barnes estate.

Sounds like they're playing my song. "Hey, is there a problem with the haunted house? Maybe I should ride along."

Erick raises his eyebrows, but it's Deputy Paulsen who answers. "Sure, Moon. You can ride in the back of the squad car."

"Never mind. I'll follow you in my car." It hasn't been that long since I had to ride in the back of the patrol car—for real—and I'm not eager to repeat the experience.

Once we hit the highway, Paulsen flips on her lights and siren and leaves me in the dust. Part of me would love to exceed the speed limit and prove to her that I can keep up, but I think we all know that would end badly.

When I reach the mansion, I'm surprised to see

Chiffon Cheryl and her publicist arguing vehemently with Erick.

Rather than rush straight into the fray, I meander along the pathway and drop some serious eaves.

Cheryl steps in front of her publicist and physically pushes her back a couple of feet as she verbally attacks Erick. "Listen, you local yokel! That doorman accosted me. I was defending myself and attempting to explain that I have every right to be here and see what my readers will experience after the book signing, but he simply wouldn't listen. He physically accosted me!"

Catching Erick's eye, I shake my head. I know he's lived in town a lot longer than me, but I feel as though I have a better understanding of Clyde. He may be more deliberate in his actions than most, and he does need to have things a certain way, but I've never seen any hint that he's violent.

Clyde's red face peeks out of the front doorway, his frustration transforming his features from gentle doorman to mildly terrifying bouncer. "She's not supposed to be here! She's not on the list!"

Maybe I spoke too soon.

The door widens, and Mrs. Charles yanks Clyde back into the house. She rushes out and slams the door behind her. "Sheriff Harper, I've known you since you were in diapers." The matronly woman pauses as she negotiates the broad granite steps.

It's a strange opening, and I feel the mention of diapers is unnecessary, but let's see where she's going.

"You and Clyde went to school together. You know he's nothing more than a gentle giant. He was simply doing his job, and this woman rudely refused to listen to reason." Now that Mrs. Charles is on the pathway, she's moving at a rapid rate toward Cheryl.

Cheryl turns to face the advancing mother and shakes her finger sharply. "No one is going to believe a word you say. Mothers always think the best of their children, no matter how stupid or useless they might be!"

At the utterance of the word "stupid," a vengeful fire ignites in Mrs. Charles' eyes. She lunges toward Cheryl and jabs her finger firmly into the pompous writer's chest—repeatedly. "Don't. You. Ever. Call. My. Son. Stupid." And once she's finished jabbing her finger, she ends her tirade with a slap across Cheryl's face.

From where I'm standing, I feel like Erick could have intercepted the act. Maybe he thought Cheryl had it coming . . . Either way, he separates the two women now and informs Cheryl that she is no longer welcome on the property.

"You and your publicist are to remove yourselves from the estate at once. If you return to this property at any time in the future, Mrs. Charles is well within her rights as caretaker of the estate to call the authorities and have you arrested for trespassing. Do I make myself clear?"

And here's the big difference between Cheryl and me. Cheryl takes one look at the matter-of-fact lawman, backs up, and nods like a simpering pup. I, on the other hand, would've taken a step toward the sheriff and told him exactly what I thought of his trespassing warning. In this case, I'm glad Cheryl and Janet agree to cooperate. I don't want some foolish misunderstanding to derail the haunted house and all the important funds it will raise for the community.

When Cheryl turns, she catches sight of me and stops short.

Blerg. I better cook up a story fast! "Cheryl! I'm so glad I ran into you. I didn't see you at the bookshop, and something told me you and Janet may have headed out here. Did you look at the haunted house?" It wasn't my best fabrication, but I'll give it a four out of ten.

Cheryl flicks her auburn waves over her shoulder and scoffs. "If I didn't already have a mountain of RSVPs for the book launch, I'd cancel everything and leave this backwater town."

Even though I prefer that option, I have to make nice for the sake of all the loyal cookbook fans who are looking forward to hearing this self-important woman spew her nonsense. "Oh, Cheryl, don't let one misunderstanding ruin your beautiful book launch. I'm sure your fans will be terribly disappointed if you cancel the event. Why not let me bring in some extra catering and really make it special?"

At the mention of catering, Janet steps forward. "No, thank you, Miss Moon. I have specifically ordered the items we'll be serving at the book launch. Each pastry was specially selected from the new cookbook and will be prepared according to Cheryl's recipes. I don't want our guests having any other food. It just wouldn't be acceptable at our cookbook launch."

Cheryl's head whip pans to the left, and she scowls fiercely at Janet. "I'm sure you mean *my* cookbook launch, Janet."

Janet seems to shrink before my eyes and bows her head submissively. "Of course, Cheryl. Of course that's what I meant."

Before I can offer any other *UN*-acceptable solutions, Cheryl and Janet brush past me and hop into their waiting car.

Paulsen has already entered the mansion to get

Clyde's statement, with Mrs. Charles hot on her heels.

Erick attempts to scrape a loose swath of his sexy blond bangs back into the pomade holding his hair in place. "You're going to have your hands full with that one, Moon. How did you get roped into hosting her book launch?"

"Don't ask me. I mean, I am the only bookshop in town, but I have no idea why she picked this town. Twiggy handled everything, so I don't know the details. Cheryl seems to think she's quite a huge deal. I'm honestly surprised she didn't want to hold her book launch in a big city like Chicago."

Erick shrugs. "Hopefully, she doesn't return to the estate. She's not part of the group that will be coming out here tomorrow night for the soft opening, is she?"

"No. That much I do know. When Twiggy offered them spots on the bus, they adamantly refused."

Erick shrugs and chuckles. "That seems to fit with the entitled tantrum we just observed. I'm gonna head inside and make sure Clyde is okay. You want me to stop by later? I could bring some dinner, or we could go out for Chinese."

"Actually, that would be perfect." It's impossible to hide the sly grin spreading across my face.

"What have you got up your sleeve?"

"Nothing. I swear. I'm just amusing myself with the zombie wedding imagery. Grams is likely to blow an ethereal circuit!"

Erick rolls his eyes. "Sweet-and-sour chicken?"

"Perfect. I'll head back into town and get a dose of Odell's french fries. A woman can't survive on Chinese food alone."

His shoulders shake with laughter as he climbs the steps to join Paulsen inside.

I load into the Jeep and drive toward the diner. Now I won't simply poke my head in to offer a good morning. I'll be sliding into a booth to enjoy the best grub in town.

CHAPTER 4

THE BREAKFAST CROWDS have long since vanished, and it will be another hour before hunger brings the lunch seekers. Taking advantage of the lull, the world's best waitress, Tally, hurriedly sweeps the black-and-white checkered floor. Each of the red-vinyl bench seats in the booths already gleams from a fresh wipe-down, and my grandfather offers me a spatula salute through the red-Formica-trimmed orders-up window. "Chili cheese fries and a chocolate malt sound good?"

Shaking my head as I chuckle, I take a seat at the counter. "Nobody likes a showoff, Gramps." Turns out there's a touch of psychic ability trickling through the sap on both sides of my family tree. Although, it must've skipped a generation, because my father doesn't seem to share any of the abilities Odell, Isadora, and I have displayed.

Deep wrinkles in Odell's face crinkle as he smiles broadly and proceeds to make exactly what he knows I want. Echoes of hot oil sizzle from the kitchen as he drops down a basket of fries.

Tally returns her broom to the back and whips up a most delicious-looking chocolate malt. "Tatum's coming home for the weekend, you know. I got us both tickets to your haunted house."

"That's fantastic, but I could've gotten you tickets at no charge. You should've let me know."

She waves away my suggestion as though it's utterly ridiculous. "Oh, pshaw. You know what my brother Ledo would do to us if he heard I didn't support the fundraiser for the animal shelter."

We share a chuckle, and I nod. "True. Doc Ledo has the biggest heart of anyone I've ever met, and he certainly picked the right profession when he became a veterinarian. I don't know what Pyewacket would do without him. I've lost count of how many times he's saved that fiendish caracal from disaster."

Tally nods her tightly wound, flame-red bun and pats her chest. "He's done a lot of good for this community. And he sure is pleased you've picked up the fundraising torch. He said this is sure to be the best event in decades, dontcha know."

She slides my malt in front of me, and my mouth waters in anticipation. "Thank you. For the compliment and the malt."

"You betcha." She laughs and heads off to refill the ketchup bottles at each table.

The first slurp is always the best. The taste of the malt powder takes me back in time—suddenly, I'm nine—and in the hot Phoenix summers, popsicles and ice cream were a girl's best friend. Before my mother passed away, she used to make sure we had one or the other at least once a week. Popsicles were fairly easy to come by, but, on our budget, malts were considered a luxury.

I remember the first time she explained the difference between a shake and a malt. Something about that added ingredient changed my whole relationship with frosty ice cream treats. Now that she's gone, I think of my loving mama every time I order a malt.

"Where'd you drift off to, kid?"

Odell's nearness makes me jump. "I didn't hear you! Well, I—"

He leans across the counter and pats my shoulder. "It's all right, Mitzy. Everyone's allowed to slip away occasionally."

As his kind words soothe my startled spirit, I recall some wise words from another important person in my life. "Odell, you got a minute?"

He walks around the counter and lowers himself onto the stool next to me. "You know I always have time for you. What's up?"

"Silas told me it's important to speak the names of the dead. He said talking about them keeps their memory alive. I just wanted to tell you where I went. I was thinking about my mother. Coraline Moon. She used to take me out for malts every once in a while, when I was a little girl. The taste always reminds me of her. I wish you could've met her. She would have . . ."

Odell slips an arm around my shoulder and hugs me close. "If she was even half as amazing as the daughter she raised, I assure you the loss was all mine. Thanks for telling me about her. I think Silas is right." He leans a little closer and whispers in my ear. "Although I kinda prefer the Myrtle Isadora method of remembering the deceased." He winks and chuckles.

Ever since he entered the inner circle of folks who know about my grandmother's ghost being permanently tethered to my bookshop, he's been a lot less curmudgeonly.

Twiggy once said Myrtle Isadora was Odell's one true love, and the fact that he never remarried was proof. I didn't have much of an opinion on the matter until I decided to let him in on our little secret last Christmas. The change in Grams and in Odell is tangible. She pesters me less about clothing, and he actually smiles more than ten percent of the time.

Odell returns to the kitchen to prepare my chili cheese fries, and I'm not ashamed to say I power through them and my malt in mere minutes.

"I better head back to the bookshop. See ya for breakfast tomorrow morning, Gramps."

He nods, and his metal spatula scrapes across the grill as he preps for the lunch rush.

Normally I blast into the bookstore, guns blazing and shouting for Grams. But on the off chance Cheryl and Janet are here, I control myself. Difficult as it is.

Carefully stepping over the "No Admittance" chain at the bottom of the wrought-iron circular staircase, I head up to my apartment. Striding through the Rare Books Loft, I drag my fingers along the edge of the perfectly aligned oak reading tables as I inhale the scent of mystery and knowledge.

Reaching up to the candle sconce on the wall, I tilt it down and wait for the secret bookcase door to slide open and reveal my safe haven.

Before I can step in and unwind, a hyperactive ghost blasts through the wall and zooms so close to me that I can feel her energy tingling against my face. "Mitzy! You have a package. Twiggy brought it up. And I was so excited I couldn't get enough corporeal form to open it."

"Good morning to you too, Grams. I don't know if we discussed it or not, but you do not have permission to open my packages. I can barely keep you from dropping into my head and reading my thoughts at will. The last thing I need is for you to start physically snooping through my belongings!" I cross my arms and fix her with my most threatening stare.

"Oh, Mitzy. Don't act like it's a federal offense." She scoffs and looks away.

"Um, that's exactly what it is! Would you like me to call the postmaster and report your ghost crime?" My false fierceness is crumbling under the absurdity of this debate.

She floats backward and clutches one of her several strands of pearls. "Well, I never!"

"Never what? Snooped or thought-dropped? We both know that's not true." Giggling, I uncross my arms and visually scan the room for the contraband. "Now, where's this package you got yourself all fired up about?"

She races toward the coffee table and points with her glowing finger. "Here! Right here."

Taking one look at the large box, I know what it

contains. However, using the trick I learned about keeping my mind blank, I rob her of the ability to steal the information from my brain.

"Mitzy! I can't believe you're playing such tricks on me."

"Maybe. Or maybe you're mad at me because I'm not letting you read my mind. Wow! Things really are upside down in your little ghost world, Grams."

We both chuckle, and I walk past the box toward my large antique four-poster bed, to have a lie down and digest my mid-morning snack.

"Aren't you going to open it?"

"Nope. I'll wait until Erick stops by tonight."

Her aura doubles its glow. "What? Isn't it bad luck for—?"

I cease my pillow fluffing and narrow my gaze.

She throws a ring-ensconced hand over her mouth, and her ghostly eyes widen.

"What were you going to say? I didn't interrupt you, but something must've stopped you. Please continue."

Keeping her hand in place, she shakes her head and mumbles, "Oh, nothing. I have some business in the museum."

And with that, she vanishes from my sight with an almost electrical ZAP.

If you're keeping score, that's Mitzy: 1; Grams: 0.

I know one thing for sure, it's going to be bad luck for *someone* when she sees that wedding dress!

CHAPTER 5

THE ONLY THING worse than being awakened from a glorious nap is being awakened by fiendish feline breath, hot on your cheek.

"Pyewacket! I don't go snooping around the bookcases rousting you from your many snoozes!"

"RE-OW!" Game on!

It's no use fighting the inevitable. If this half-wild caracal wants something, he won't give up until he gets it. Pushing myself into a sitting position on the luxurious comforter, I rub my eyes and rake loose fingers through my snow-white hair. "All right. I'm up. What's your urgent business, your royal furriness?"

The black tufts on his sharply pointed ears flick back and forth. He extends the needle-like claws on his forefoot, skewers a sheet of paper, and shoves it toward me.

Taking the offering, I examine it carefully. "Hey! This is a page from one of those new cookbooks for the launch party! Now I'm going to have to pay for it, Pye. Yeesh!"

To be fair, he may have a strange way of communicating, but he's seldom wrong. Taking a second look at the sheet of paper, I note it's a recipe titled Chocolate Chip and Pin Cherry Scones. This has to be the scone recipe Chiffon Cheryl allegedly stole from Anne. I know next to nothing about baking, so all the ingredients seem standard to me. "There's no official crime, Pyewacket, but consider it logged into evidence, regardless. It wouldn't be the first time you were one or two steps ahead of me."

"Reow." Can confirm.

Finally reaching fully alert, I remember this evening's special guest. "If you need anything, run downstairs and bug Twiggy. I have to take a shower and make myself beautiful for Erick."

If cats could chuckle—

"Hey, I'm not sure I care for that sound, Mr. Cuddlekins. I'll deal with you later."

He squeezes his eyelids to near slits and flops onto the bed with absolute disregard for my warning.

The indescribable glories of a fully functional shower with steaming-hot water, stocked with euca-lyptus bath products, never cease to calm me. Back in my nearly condemned apartment in Sedona, I was lucky to get three solid minutes of tepid sput-tering, followed by a freezing blast. I may have hit the jackpot when Grams left me her estate, but I'll never forget where I came from.

When I step out of the shower, I indulge myself in two luxurious Egyptian cotton bath towels; one wrapped snugly around my wet hair and the other around my body.

I'll start with the makeup and work my way up to a hairdo.

As I apply my simple pallet of colors, memories of my mother once again rocket to the forefront. I can almost hear her voice . . . Twice in one day? What's going on?

Without a moment's hesitation, I seek out my cell phone and call the one person who literally has all the answers. "Good afternoon, Mr. Willoughby. How are you doing?"

He harrumphs loudly, and I can easily picture him smoothing his bushy grey mustache with thumb and forefinger. "Good afternoon, Mitzy. To what do I owe the pleasure of this call?"

Best get straight to the point. My alchemical mentor doesn't suffer fools. "I had two weird incidents today. Both involved extremely detailed memories of my mother. Smells, tastes, the whole deal. Is it some kind of sign?"

"Indeed. But not in the way you may assume."

Leave it to Silas to make even the simplest of answers cryptic. "Care to elaborate?"

"Certainly. As we approach All Hallows' Eve, or Samhain as it was known to the Celts, the veil between the worlds becomes quite thin. You may notice your grandmother's ghost acting strangely as well, as spirits from the other side become more discernible."

"Discernible? Like how?"

As I finish applying my mascara, I can almost feel my mother's lips kiss the tip of my nose, as she did so many times in my youth. A quiet gasp escapes my lips, but fortunately doesn't interrupt Silas.

"It refers to the ability of spirits on the other side of the veil to reach out to loved ones with messages and signs."

"Like malts?"

Silas guffaws; the length of his laughter surely must cause his cheeks to redden. I look forward to the next time I'm able to see him in person.

While he composes himself, I plow ahead. "So, is it possible my mother is trying to communicate with me?"

He exhales loudly. "It is far more than a potential likelihood, Mizithra. It is nearly certain. A mother's love for her child is one of the most powerful forces on earth—as well as in the great beyond. It would be plausible for your mother to use every means at her disposal to reach you."

"Silas, how can I help her? I want her to reach me. More than anything."

He inhales sharply. "There is a way, but it is more difficult than you would imagine."

"Tell me. Anything. Absolutely anything!"

A heavy silence hangs between us, and I know better than to break it. Eventually, there is a rustling, and I exhale the breath I didn't realize I've been holding.

"It would be possible to conduct a séance. In this way, you would open yourself up to the spirit realm and create a space for her to leak briefly into our world."

"I'll do it—right now!"

"It would be prudent to wait until the full moon. There will be less—interference. However, you must understand the risks."

"Come on, Silas. You know me. Risk is my middle name."

At this, he fails to laugh. "I would disagree. I believe your middle name to be foolhardy, or perhaps overconfident."

Ouch! "Fine. What are the risks?"

"A psychic, such as yourself, possesses many senses beyond those of an average human. While you make a wonderful conduit to the netherworld, there can be dire consequences."

His tone of voice disheartens me, and I sink to the floor, leaving the phone on the counter, on speaker. "Like what?"

"Most precisely, your mother is not the only spirit struggling to get a message through the barrier. When you open yourself up, other information is likely to seep through."

"That's okay. I can handle more than one message."

"Not all spirits are benign, Mizithra. When you open yourself up to the messages of those who've passed beyond this realm, you open yourself up to potential harm. There are malevolent spirits who wish to wreak havoc in our world. You may provide them with precisely the window they seek."

He's used my formal name, and that's supposed to warn me of the seriousness of his words. "But, Silas! I need to speak to my mother. There has to be something we can do. Aren't there some protections you could put in place?" My palms are sweating, and I'm afraid tears may leak out and spoil my carefully applied mascara.

"As always, I shall carefully research your request. We are fortunate to have a measure of time before the full moon. Once I have the appropriate information, I shall contact you."

"Thank you, Silas. It's so important to me. Honestly, I can't thank you enough."

After coaxing my stubborn locks into a semblance of a hairdo, I slip on a robe and set up the rest of the items for the prank. When I officially don the costume, and wear it to host the haunted house, I'll put serious effort into some movie-realistic zombie makeup. For the prank on Grams, I'm using a passable mask.

BING. BONG. BING.

"He's here!"

I swoop out of the apartment and down the circular staircase. Yes, I tempt fate and try to hop over the chain at the bottom. And, also yes, I fail miserably. The toe of my trailing foot catches, and I launch forward in a Three-Stooges-style stumble.

Lucky for me, Twiggy left early to attend a special bingo night. My pratfall remains cackle-free.

However, before I can make it to the alleyway door, Grams blasts through the wall separating my bookshop from the adjacent printing museum. "Is it Erick? Or Odell? Either way, I need to have a chat."

Throwing myself into my role, I place a fist on one hip and shake a finger in her general direction. "Listen, Isadora, it's Erick. I need a few minutes alone with my boyfriend. However, if you play nice and give me fifteen uninterrupted minutes, we'll allow you to join us in the apartment for a quick chat before Erick and I head out for sweet-and-sour chicken."

She attempts to arch an eyebrow and look cross, but she's so desperate to talk to Erick that she takes the bait. "Fine, I'll be on the third floor working on my—"

"Your NOT memoirs?"

Her eyes widen, and she vanishes through the wall before I can rehash the standing argument about her little white lie. Turns out she isn't writing her memoirs at all! She is happily planning to share each and every personal detail of my life with her imagined readership.

Once she's gone, I race to the back door and scoop Erick inside as quickly as possible. "Hurry up. We only have fifteen minutes."

He tilts his head and arches an eyebrow. "I'll do my best, but fifteen minutes doesn't give a guy much time."

My jaw drops like a broken rock 'em sock 'em robot. "Sheriff Harper! Do not twist my words for your nefarious purposes. You know what I'm talking about. Now hustle upstairs. Step it out, soldier!"

He laughs openly at my attempt to be commanding and glides over the chain at the bottom of the staircase with ease. Taking my time, I carefully join him and we rush into my apartment.

"All right. I have the dress and the mask—and everything ready. I'll put it on and strike a pose facing away from the door. When she enters, I'll say something about the dress to signal you. Then you can pretend you hate it, or whatever you want. I'll take a beat—and turn. I'll let you know when she's done screaming!"

He shrugs. "Whatever you say, *dear*. I still can't believe you're going to all this trouble for a joke. But I suppose you heiresses have extra time on your hands."

"Oh brother. Don't start with me, Sheriff. We all have moments when we abuse our power." I flash my eyebrows, and his gaze immediately shifts to the floor.

Hustling into the bathroom, I slip into the dress, secure the mask over my face, and slip the veil onto my head. The dead flowers at the crown, and the bouquet of equally deceased flowers in my hand, complete the ruse.

When I walk out, Erick jumps back in a moment of genuine fear. "That's creepy."

"That's perfect. Save it for the surprise!" Turning my back to the secret door, I strike a pose that hides my dead floral arrangement.

Erick and I wait with somewhat bated breath.

Right on time, Ghost-ma phases through the bookcase.

Now to toss out the signal. "Do you really think so, Erick?"

Wait for it . . .

"Oh, Mitzy! Why would you choose such a dingy shade of grey? Oh, no! Erick isn't supposed to—"

Before Isadora can finish her tirade, I slowly turn and stretch my zombie arms toward her.

She shrieks in true ghostly horror, and the color fades from her like a washed-out film negative. Her burgundy silk-and-tulle Marchesa gown instantly shifts to a shabby shade of grey.

To his credit, even though Erick can't see her, he continues to play along until I break.

Laughter consumes me, and I slip off the mask. "Gotcha! And that's what you get for spying on me when I'm shopping. When I have the need to buy an actual wedding dress, I will happily include you."

Her coloring flickers and begins to refill, as though someone is hand coloring a vintage photograph. "Mizithra! How dare you!"

"How dare I? I'll tell you how I dare. You never stop pushing the boundaries of my privacy. You should know better. As you're well aware, I have a large streak of 'Ghost-ma' running through my veins. I love having you here in the bookshop. I would never want it any other way. Although there are some things I would like to keep to myself."

Erick uncomfortably clears his throat. "Uh, I'm feeling like a third wheel over here."

"Sorry, Erick. This conversation with Grams was long overdue." Turning to Ghost-ma, I offer her an olive branch. "I tell you what: I absolutely promise that if you double-down on your efforts to stay out of my mind and cease your endless thought-dropping, I will allow you to begin planning the perfect wedding dress."

Her shade shoots to Technicolor, and I fear she might explode.

"Hold on! To be clear, there's no reason for it, no engagement, and no date, but I want you to have plenty of time."

My paranormally impaired boyfriend glances at me and tilts his head—a mixture of curiosity and concern.

I shrug my shoulders and exhale. What can I say to him? I'm spitballing here!

Grams zooms toward me and throws her ethereal arms around my shoulders. The first time this happened, I found it quite unsettling, but now I've grown used to the loving sensation of her prickly energy enveloping me. "Oh, Mitzy! You really are the best granddaughter in the entire universe! I'm so glad you put me in charge. You know this is one of my areas of specialty!"

Extracting myself from her energy, I attempt to hide my smirk. "You don't say, Myrtle Isadora Johnson Linder Duncan Willamet Rogers."

She gasps and toys with the idea of protesting, but in the end, we both collapse in a fit of giggles.

"Well, once again, gals, feeling like an extra snowflake in a blizzard."

"Sorry! I got a little carried away. Let me change into an actual outfit, and then we can grab some dinner."

As I turn toward the closet, Grams' glowing finger taps me on the shoulder. When I look back, she has her hands pressed together in prayer pose.

"Yes, you can pick out my outfit!"

Erick chuckles and flops onto the over-stuffed settee.

Grams and I head into the closet—one of us through the wall and one through the doorway. Now that she knows the dress is only for my Halloween costume, she's over the moon. No pun intended.

CHAPTER 6

TO STEAL A PHRASE FROM CAT STEVENS, morning has broken. Don't blame me. My mother had a very eclectic taste in music. I'd love to roll over and snuggle with my overnight guest, but the ever-present Pyewacket is stretched out between us like a Victorian chaperone.

Peeking over the large mass of tan fur, I smile wickedly as my defenseless boyfriend sleeps as though he hasn't a care in the world.

Slowly stretching my hand toward his tousled blond head, I giggle silently, intent on flicking his ear.

Robin Pyewacket Goodfellow has other plans. A large paw shoots into the air and swats my hand away from Sheriff Too-Hot-To-Handle.

"Rude. Remember who fills your food bowl, son."

Pyewacket utters an entirely new vocal intonation and nuzzles his tufted ears against Erick's exposed chest.

That's it. Sitting up in a huff, I exit the bed and mumble "traitor" under my breath. It won't take me long to slip into my skinny jeans and a snarky tee.

Grams has honored our privacy and is nowhere to be found. She doesn't even pop into my *Sex and the City* meets *Confessions of a Shopaholic* closet to insist on me wearing something other than a T-shirt.

When I emerge from the spacious walk-in monument to couture, Erick is slipping his feet into his tactical boots. He looks up with a mouthwatering grin that shifts into confusion. "Are you serious with that T-shirt?"

I look down. There are three crooked tombstones and the tagline, "Never trust the living." "Dead serious, Sheriff. Now let's get to breakfast before all the best seats are taken."

He hops up and helps me with my jacket and my striped scarf. "What do you always say? Copy that?"

"10-4, Sheriff."

He rolls his big blue eyes. "Did you get into Hogwarts?"

Scrunching up my face, I shake my head. "What are you talking about?"

"That scarf looks like a dead ringer for Harry Potter's."

I run my hands over the plush maroon and gold stripes and chuckle. "Don't let Grams hear you say that. I'm sure it's some fancy schmancy cashmere or something. It's soft, and I like it. But now that you mention it . . ." I wave my hand as though it holds an imaginary wand, and we both smirk.

He presses the twisted ivy medallion on the wall that opens the hidden bookcase from inside the apartment. As he walks into the Rare Books Loft, he stops and swoops me behind him with his left arm. Turning, he silently points towards the glowing green-glass lampshade on the oak reading table in the corner.

My heart stutters, but before I completely freak out, I recognize the way the light is glinting off the bald pate of the chair's occupant. "Good morning, Silas."

He inhales sharply and turns with some effort. "Ah, good morning Mitzy and guest."

Erick sighs comically. "I'd like to think I'm special enough to have a name, Mr. Willoughby."

Silas chuckles and smooths his bushy mustache. "Indeed. You are singular in that regard, Mr. Harper."

Erick laughs as though the comment means nothing, but my extra senses pick up on the quickening of his heartbeat and the soupçon of pride radiating from his broad shoulders.

"Erick and I are headed to the diner for breakfast. Do you want to join us?"

"Too late, I'm afraid. I was up at dawn and enjoyed breaking my fast in my sunroom prior to driving into town."

Shrugging, I head for the spiral staircase. "Your loss."

Erick follows, but pauses and turns toward my attorney/alchemist. "You seem to be into some very serious research, Silas. What are you working on?"

Silas grumbles and sniffs sharply. His milky-blue eyes seem to sharpen as he stares in my direction. "I assumed Mizithra had shared her intention to host a séance. I'm simply endeavoring to deduce the safest possible method."

My stunned boyfriend leans back and rubs his hand over his open mouth. "A séance? You're not serious?"

Silas harrumphs. "I should think you know me well enough to understand I'm not a man to jest, Sheriff."

Erick shakes his head and shoots a sideways glance in my direction.

Rather than stick around for the third degree, I

hustle down the stairs and purposely unhook the chain. "Better hurry up, Sheriff. The alarm goes off in thirty."

He bounds down the stairs with ease and secures the chain behind him.

The blustery day that greets us outside carries an unexpected bone-chilling edge. Using the circumstances to my advantage, I break into a light jog and make for the diner.

He easily keeps pace with me and arrives in time to hold the door.

When we step inside, Odell offers me a wink and gestures toward the corner booth.

We slip onto opposite red-vinyl bench seats and gladly accept the steaming mugs of coffee that follow right behind us.

Erick walks his fingers across the table and turns up his palm. I eagerly place my hand in his, and realize too late—it's a trap.

He squeezes my hand and offers me a stern look. "A séance, Mitzy. What on earth are you up to now?"

I toy with the idea of making up a story, but we've come so far and worked so hard to get to a place where we can be honest with one another. I immediately shove that idea away and plow ahead. "My mother's been attempting to contact me from beyond the veil. I don't know what she wants, but I have to talk to her.

This time of year is an especially effective time to communicate with spirits who have crossed over."

He tilts his head, swallows, and opens his mouth to speak.

I hold out my finger. "Don't ask how I know that. I'm only repeating what Silas told me."

Erick nods and gestures for me to continue.

"Holding a séance is a way to create a safe space for her to communicate with me and open myself up to receive the messages. Silas is looking into how to get it done."

He rubs his thumb across the back of my hand and momentarily bites his bottom lip. "Okay. But I heard him use the word 'safe.' Is there some risk involved in holding a séance?"

This is the part in the story where I almost always stretch the truth. Deep breath, Mitzy. Deep breath. "Because of my abilities, Silas thinks that if I open myself up to receive messages from my mother, other spirits might try to get through."

Erick nods. "That makes sense. Well, as much as any of this makes sense. What's the harm in getting a few extra messages?"

Swallowing with difficulty, I squeeze his hand for courage and continue. "Not all spirits are benevolent."

It takes a moment for the true magnitude of my

words to bounce through the intricate pathways of his brain. "Oh. That sounds dangerous. Maybe you shouldn't do it."

"Erick. You have to understand what it would mean for me to be able to speak to my mother. I know you don't quite get it because your mom is still around. But if she weren't—"

"Don't even say that, Mitzy."

"No. No. I'm not wishing anyone harm. I'm just asking you to imagine—*if she weren't*—wouldn't you be willing to try anything just to hear her voice again?" My throat clenches up at the end of the sentence, and big tears drip from the corners of my eyes.

Right on schedule, Odell approaches the table with our plates but stops in mid-delivery. "Hey, I don't like to see tears in my granddaughter's eyes, Harper. What's going on?"

Without missing a beat, Erick spills the whole séance story, risks and all. Odell sets down our plates and slides into the booth next to me. "I see both sides, kids. Erick is right to be concerned for your safety, Mitzy. But I would've tried anything to speak to Isadora." He roughly clears his throat, pats my shoulder, and disappears into the kitchen.

Erick exhales loudly, and his shoulders slump. "You win. But I want to be there."

"You do? Oh, Erick. That's awesome! My mom is gonna absolutely freak. I mean, in a good way."

My mom is gonna meet my boyfriend! Technically, my mom's ghost, but po-tay-to, po-tah-to.

If I thought séance talk at breakfast was the most interesting thing that would happen this morning—

Things take a fascinating turn before I can even finish my delicious fare.

And you know that doesn't take long.

Chiffon Cheryl and her mousy assistant burst through the door, turn sharply, and immediately take the four-top by the front window.

They certainly don't notice me, or any of their surroundings. They each pick up a menu and stare in silence. The tension between them is palpable—especially to someone with psychic senses. Leaning across the table, I lower my voice and whisper. "The celebrity cookbook author from yesterday's kerfuffle just walked in. It sure looks like she and her assistant are having some kind of tiff."

Erick casually glances over his shoulder and shrugs. "You might be reading too much into it. Maybe they're not morning people. Once they get a cup of coffee in them, it might change their whole attitude."

I'm not going to wave my extra sensory perceptions in his face, but I'm certain a cup of coffee isn't going to fix whatever's going on over there.

Janet makes a comment, and Cheryl slams her hand down on the table.

I quickly sink into my psychic abilities and can now hear the conversation as though I'm seated at the table with them. Janet is speaking through gritted teeth. "All I'm asking for is some respect. I do everything for you. I even talked the publisher into paying for this foolish book launch in this backwater town just so you could stick it to some imagined rival. I'm telling you, that woman at Bless Choux barely knows you're alive."

Cheryl jabs a finger in Janet's direction. "Don't take that tone with me. You're well-compensated for your services."

Janet leans forward, and the snarl that grips her features transforms her from mousy to dangerous in the blink of an eye. "I'll take whatever tone I want, Chiffon. Don't forget, I know exactly where all your secret recipes came from." Janet leans back in her chair and crosses her arms over her chest. Her gaze instantly falls to the floor.

If I were seated across from her, I'd cut my losses and order breakfast, but Cheryl is not that kind of woman. She drops her menu and growls. "And you best not forget, I pulled you up from the gutter and gave you the opportunity of a lifetime. Assistants are a dime a dozen. Don't test me, *Janet*."

And with that, Cheryl picks up her menu, flicks it sharply, and snaps her fingers rudely in Tally's direction.

Not on my watch. I grip the edge of the table and prepare to launch myself from the booth, but Erick's firm hand grips my shoulder. "Hey, I don't know where you went, but why don't you take a deep breath and tell me what's going on?"

He's right. Making a scene will get me nowhere. I fill him in on the conversation I overheard. ". . . and the way she said Janet's name. I tell you what, I could never work for a woman like that."

"Well, lucky for you, Moon. You never have to work for anyone again. But I do remember you once had to answer to someone you called SUPER-visor Dean."

His reference to my dark days in Sedona brings an instant chuckle. "I've never met a man so excited about serving coffee."

Erick grins. "And you weren't excited about coffee?"

"Only about drinking it."

He leans back and makes room for Tally to refill our mugs with some hot java.

"I don't think it's the coffee you have a problem with. I think you like to be in control, Moon."

Tally attempts to keep it professional. But I hear her snicker as she hustles to put the coffeepot back on the warmer behind the counter.

"I heard that, Tally."

My outburst draws Janet's attention. As soon as she lays eyes on me, her shoulders droop and she casts her gaze to the floor.

Does she find me intimidating? Or did she just realize she's in a public place? I honestly don't know, and I lean hard into my psychic senses for extra information.

"Hey, I better go say good morning to my special guest, and hurry back to the bookshop to pretend to help Twiggy."

Erick nods. "Enjoy your book signing. At least there will be some delicious pastries, right?"

I roll my eyes. "I'm sure none of them could hold a candle to Anne's!" As I slide toward the end of the booth, I ask one more question. "Hey, did you still want to come to the soft opening of the haunted house tonight?"

He rubs his left thumb along his jawline and shrugs. "Do I want to? Not necessarily, but it feels like the right boyfriend move."

"Look, I'll make it easy for you. You can come dressed as a sheriff. We'll save the zombie groom costume and the full movie makeup for All Hallows' Eve. Deal?"

He nods. "Deal."

Leaving him in the booth to finish his coffee, I casually approach Cheryl's table. "Good morning, ladies. Enjoy your breakfast, and we'll see you around four o'clock. Please let me know if there are any changes that need to be made."

Janet nods mutely.

Cheryl gazes up through her thick false eyelashes and pastes on a large, fraudulent smile. "Thank you so much, Mitzy. We're really looking forward to it."

I've got to get out of the diner before this woman's terrible performance brings up my breakfast. "See you later."

And with that, I'm out.

CHAPTER 7

AFTER SEVERAL HOURS of attempting to assist Twiggy with the book launch preparations, she dismisses me in a huff. "Look, kid, I appreciate you making an effort and all, but it takes me twice as long to explain to you what to do as it would take me to just get it done. So, why don't you head up top and make sure your grams doesn't pull one of her stunts tonight? I'll take care of everything down here."

"Copy that. What are we supposed to do with the extra cookbooks? I mean, what's left over after the book signing?"

Twiggy stomps one of her signature biker boots and slaps her hand on the thigh of her dungarees. "Left over! Doll, you've honestly got no idea how self-important this woman is. Apparently, she's got tens of thousands of social media followers, and when she mentioned this quaint venue and the limited number of tickets, we sold out in minutes. There aren't any leftover cookbooks. As a matter of fact, I hope somebody is a no-show, because one of these precious tomes has a missing page."

I gulp, and my eyes widen.

"Don't worry, Your Highness. I saw the claw marks. I'm not placing blame on you. Between that furry fiend and our resident ghost, we'll be lucky if a missing page is the only thing that goes wrong tonight."

"Thanks for everything you did to pull this all together. I know you already know it, but I feel like I don't say it often enough. I could never run this place without you."

For a split second, her defenses lower and a smile touches her feisty dark-brown eyes. "We all have our crosses to bear."

Departing with a chuckle, I push the bar on the "Employees Only" door and step into the printing museum. The smells of old machinery, ink, and history have their usual effect. However, before I take two steps toward our authentic Gutenberg, a vision grips me so fiercely that I'm forced to drop immediately to the ground.

The equipment vanishes, and the surrounding space becomes a large open-plan kitchen, with an enormous living room and formal dining room. There's a gorgeous fireplace in the living room, and I can feel the heat of the crackling flames on my cheeks.

Is this some kind of lucid dreaming? I can barely remember how Silas described it to me, but if it's what I think it is, I should be able to walk through it and see more.

Rising, I stumble forward, and crack my knee on the Gutenberg. The vision temporarily falters as I bite back an expletive and rub my kneecap, but I take several deep breaths and restore it to as solid as it previously was. Moving slowly, I head for the stairs.

On the second floor, there are two gorgeous guestrooms with en suite and sizable closets. There's also a small sitting area next to a second fireplace that seems like it would make a cozy reading nook.

Continuing up the stairs to the third floor, I'm greeted by a lovely seating area, complete with floor-to-ceiling bookcases and comfy overstuffed furniture. There's a small built-in desk in the corner, but work isn't the focus of this area.

As I glide forward within the vision, the primary suite unfolds. It takes my breath away. It's so spacious and beautiful—and has its own fireplace. There's a lovely walk-in closet, not quite as big as the one in my swanky apartment, but still larger than my crappy old apartment in Sedona, Arizona. The bathroom is magnificent! A walk-in shower, a Jacuzzi tub, double vanities—

"Oh, Mitzy! What on earth are you doing? Are you still playing that zombie joke on me? Wandering around with your arms out in front of you, ignoring every single thing I say. Jokes over, sweetie. I'm genuinely worried about you."

Ghost-ma's concerned voice breaks the vision, and I turn toward her, still partially wrapped in the shock of what I've seen. "Grams, what was this before it was a printing museum?"

"Well, you know as well as I do. It was the old Iron Range Brewing Company. Cal bought the building for me, and I oversaw the remodel. I set up this area as a museum to tie into all the valuable vintage books we were collecting. It was quite popular in the beginning, but, as with any old technology, modern generations eventually lost interest. All we have now is the occasional group of students from the local elementary school traipsing through with disinterest on field trip day. Why do you ask?"

Her answer doesn't provide me with what I'd hoped. "I might've just had a vision."

She squeals with delight and rubs her hands together as she floats closer. "Oh, sweetie! Tell me everything."

I carefully describe the images to her and how real everything seemed, even the heat from the fireplaces.

Huge ghost tears well up in her ethereal eyes, and, for the first time in a long time, I remember how many times I'd promised to find a handkerchief for her afterlife weeping. "What's wrong, Grams?"

"I don't think it was a dream, dear. You had a premonition. Think about it! You and Erick are dangerously close to getting married—or at least engaged. You can't possibly live at his house, with his mother, and leave me behind. I'm stuck in this bookshop. It would make sense that you'd want to make your new home here. And I was just mentioning how underutilized the space seems. It sounds to me like you and Erick will end up remodeling this three-story museum into your dream home."

My chest feels tight, and I can't seem to get enough air. I drop into the nearest antique chair. "I don't know, Grams. When you say it like that, everything seems too real. Plus, Gracie Harper can't live on her own. Her eyesight is practically nonexistent. She's very dependent on Erick—"

Grams nods and fiddles with one of her strands of pearls. "Did you see a room for her in the vision?"

"I don't know what I saw. I can't imagine

starting my new life with Erick right under his mother's nose. Not to mention under the ever-watchful eye of the world's snoopiest ghost!"

"Mizithra!"

"Let's put it aside, Grams. It's all too much for me right now. I just want to focus on being in a happy place with Erick, and not overcomplicate it with detailed plans for the future."

"It's your prerogative."

"Thanks, Bobby Brown."

She swipes away her momentary tears and giggles maniacally. "Oh, sweetie. I get that reference. I actually get that one." She floats away, humming the hit eighties tune under her breath.

The vision-questing seems to have sapped my energy. I wander down the stairs and gaze suspiciously at everything in the printing museum. Was it a premonition? The simple daydream fantasy of a lovesick fool?

Back in the apartment, I lay out my costume so that my quick change after the book signing won't delay the people who purchased tickets to the soft opening of the haunted house.

For the book signing itself, I select grey wool slacks, black ankle boots, and a soft cashmere sweater in a lovely shade of deep purple. It's comfortable, but also keeps it professional enough for the event.

Time to head downstairs and greet the guests.

When I reach the bottom of the wrought-iron staircase, Twiggy is already checking tickets against her list and directing eager readers and bakers to their seats.

It's my understanding that Chiffon Cheryl will briefly discuss her favorite recipes, answer a handful of questions, and then set up at the signing table.

I check the stack of books and supplies, but Twiggy has everything well in hand.

Circulating through the rows of chairs, I greet the men and women who have gathered to meet their baking idol.

After what brief contact I've had with Cheryl, I would love to tell them the truth and save them two or three hours of their lives.

It's four o'clock sharp, and there's no sign of Cheryl.

Classic diva move. She probably wants to make sure everyone's anxiously fidgeting in their seats before she makes her grand entrance.

The pastry table looks quite impressive. Janet said they had the items flown in from an exclusive bakery in Chicago. Once again, why not just have the book signing in Chicago? Although, now that I overheard that snippet of conversation this morning, it seems like Cheryl specifically chose Pin Cherry Harbor simply to stick it to Anne.

One more reason for me to dislike this baking bit—

4:10. No Cheryl.

By 4:20, the guests are getting restless. I step onto the dais and walk back and forth as I offer reassurance. "Good afternoon, everyone. Thank you so much for coming to the Bell, Book & Candle. I'm the owner, Mitzy Moon, and for those of you who purchased the add-on, I'll be escorting you to the haunted house after the book signing. Cheryl should be here any minute. I can't imagine what's keeping her."

As I continue to vamp for the impatient patrons, the sudden appearance of Janet catches my eye.

"I think we're about to begin, folks." Stepping off the small raised platform, I hurry toward the anxious assistant.

"What's going on? Where's Cheryl?"

Janet grips my arm and her breath comes in short, desperate pants. "I have no idea. I've been looking for her for hours! Once Cheryl convinced Mrs. Charles to allow her to tour the haunted house, I went back to the hotel."

Based on Janet's state of agitation, it's safe to assume Cheryl wasn't in her room when Janet went to fetch her. "Have you tried her cell phone?"

Janet's panic momentarily shifts to irritation. "Of course! I'm a personal assistant, Miss Moon. I thought of everything. Called her friends. Called her ex. I even tried the 'FindMe' app, but her phone must be turned off. It's not like her to miss a public appearance."

There's something beneath the panic. It's likely a smidgen of lingering irritation from their disagreement earlier. "How would you like to proceed, Janet? I can certainly refund everyone's money, but it's my understanding some of these people flew here from quite distant locales."

She nods and taps a nervous hand on her lips. "I'm sure she'll show up any minute. Why don't I take some questions and then encourage the guests to try the pastries from the book? If she's not here to sign by then, we're sunk."

"Copy that. Let me know if there's anything I can do."

Janet exhales dramatically. "Thank you. I will."

She takes the stage, and within minutes has the audience eating out of her hand—literally.

"I'm so glad you asked the question about scones, Gladys. I have to insist that the butter be quite cold. You won't get a true scone consistency if the butter is too soft. We want a crumbly mixture.

The largest of those crumbs being no bigger than the size of a pea. The worst thing you can do is over-work scone dough. Then you'll have nothing more than a hockey puck. And no one wants that!"

The crowd nods adoringly.

Janet continues to take questions without directly looking at any of the fans as she retrieves the tray of chocolate chip and pin cherry scones and moves up and down the rows of chairs, allowing the eager guests to take samples.

She competently fields additional questions and directs the patrons to the pastry table. At this point, I'm not entirely sure it will matter whether Cheryl shows up at all.

Oops. Spoke too soon.

Turns out, it matters to a handful of attendees. However, when I comp their cookbooks and give them free passes to the haunted house—all is forgotten.

While the guests enjoy their pastries, I pull Janet aside. "What should we do? I know the local Sheriff, if you think we should be seriously concerned."

Janet's eyes dart left and right behind her glasses. She chews her bottom lip and whimpers. "I honestly don't know what to do. Sorry about that 'personal assistant' comment earlier. Cheryl has had little tantrums before, but, as I said, she's never missed a public appearance." Janet inhales sharply and exhales a shaky breath. "Maybe we should be concerned. But we can't disappoint these people any further. You have to escort them to the haunted house." She stares at me pleadingly.

I nod and give her shoulder a comforting squeeze. "Let's get them to the next stop on their adventure, and then we can all pitch in to find Cheryl. Pin Cherry Harbor isn't that big! We'll find her."

Janet smiles wistfully and wanders toward an empty chair.

I step over the chain and head up to the mezzanine. Looking down at the patrons, I clear my throat and make my announcement. "We'll be departing for the haunted house in five minutes, folks. There will be a school bus out front to take you to the attraction and bring you back to the bookshop and your vehicles after the tour."

A few smiles and a smattering of clapping.

"Let me change into my haunted hostess outfit, and we'll get going!"

Nothing. Nada. Bupkus.

Oh, gee whiz, I can't wait to take these deadbeats on my spooky adventure.

At least I'll have Erick to take my mind off the torture.

PING.

Hooray! A text from my—

"Sorry, Mitzy. Can't get away from the office. Domestic disturbance call. I need to accompany Deputy Johnson. I'll make it up. Promise."

Blerg.

CHAPTER 8

PRESTO! CHANGE-O! We're on the bus and headed for adventure. About half the group declines part two of the evening and departs directly from the bookshop.

When we pull up in front of the imposing Barnes Manor, the remaining participants softly ooh and aah.

As the guests file off the bus, one lady comments, "That's a nice dress, dear. But I don't get the mask." She descends and heads for the walkway before I can explain my apparently confusing zombie bride costume.

"Thanks for driving the bus, Artie."

The small, dark-eyed woman nods her curly head of hair and grins. "You're just lucky we didn't get an early snow this year, you know. Drivin' the snow plow always comes first, but I'm pleased as punch to support the fundraising efforts until those first flakes fall."

Grinning, I pat her on the shoulder and join the guests as they queue up in front of the manor. For the soft opening, I didn't hire the enormous Angel of Death with her imposing black wings to greet the patrons. She's booked for the Grand Opening, though! I was so impressed with her performance at Chef Mumler's gigantic party a couple of years ago that I had to track her down. Tonight, Clyde will serve his usual role as doorman.

However, the door docs not open. I move past the line of people, mount the steps, and knock firmly on the door.

There are muffled voices within, and eventually, Clyde bursts through the imposing oak door, looking quite unprofessional. His hair is mussed, and his jacket is buttoned crookedly. Or maybe it's missing a button. I can't be sure.

"Hi, Clyde. Everything all right?"

His hands shake as he shoves them behind his back. "Fine. It's fine, Miss Moon." He averts his gaze and gestures for me to enter.

I lead the way into the hall of portraits, and a few of the guests comment softly. One lady utters a hushed scream when the eyes of a nameless baron follow her across the room.

The next few rooms meet with minimal reaction, and I'm wondering if I should turn this barge around and load these unimpressed lame-Os back on the bus. Hopefully, the decorated graveyard will impress even the skeptics.

As the thick fog roils across the ground and the sounds of ghosts calling and chains rattling fill the air, the guests huddle together and move more slowly. When we reach the headstones and the coffin pops open, several ladies, and a few of the men, scream loudly.

Laughter is about to grip me, but my mood ring burns like fire on my left hand and interferes with my gloating. I look down, and once again see the page from the cookbook floating in the smoky cabochon. As I puzzle over the meaning of the image, the words *Cheryl* and *corpse* hit me with rapid fire.

I take three steps backward to reset the coffin bit and walk forward to trigger the pop-up once again. When the lid creaks open, all my psychic senses screech to life. The body in the coffin is not a fake!

Looks like I solved the mystery of the missing author, while simultaneously uncovering a new conundrum.

Who killed Chiffon Cheryl?

Directing the confused guests back into the manor, I call out for Mrs. Charles. She must be on site. I heard Clyde mumbling to someone earlier.

The visitors are restless, so I send them into the haunted library—with its sliding bookcases, whispering voices, and trick candles—and promise to catch up in a minute.

Exiting the attraction, I wander into the grand entrance and repeatedly call for Mrs. Charles.

She finally appears from a back room, but there is a smudge of dirt on her face.

"Miss Moon, is something wrong?"

"Something is very wrong, Mrs. Charles. There is an actual corpse in that coffin in the graveyard."

She smiles and waves my concern away with her hand. "Oh no. It's fine, dear. Just a very realistic prop Clyde found." Sensing the dirt on her face, she pulls a kerchief from her pocket and dabs at her left cheek.

"Where were you, Mrs. Charles? I called you several times."

"Well, I was in the kitchen, dear. I thought perhaps your guests would enjoy a refreshment after the tour."

"And the dirt on your face? Where did that come from?"

Her manner turns icy as she shoves the hand-kerchief into her pocket. "I do not care for your tone, Miss Moon. I think you and your guests should be leaving."

Reaching back to the ribbons that secure the mask over my face, I pull one firmly and catch the mask as it drops. "Oh, I won't be going anywhere."

Grabbing my phone, I immediately call Erick—on speaker. "Good evening, Sheriff. I know you had to beg off this little event because of a work thing. But I suggest you load up in your cruiser with an extra deputy or two and hustle out to the Barnes estate. And—"

Before I have a chance to spill the beans, he interrupts. "Don't tell me. There's a dead body."

"How did you know?"

"It's the corpse magnet thing, Moon. I'm on my way."

I end the call and slip the phone back into my hidden pocket.

Mrs. Charles overheard Erick's comment, and I don't care for the smug look adorning her face.

"I suggest you get your story straight before the sheriff arrives, Mrs. Charles. That body in the coffin is no prop."

Mrs. Charles' features remain stoic, but my special abilities allow me to peer beneath the surface.

She's worried and upset. It doesn't exactly feel like guilt, but I'm still learning how to interpret all these special perceptions.

With no further explanation to the caretaker, I return to the graveyard. It might've been a mistake to warn a potential suspect to get her story straight, but that horse already left the barn. I may as well take advantage of the time I have remaining before Erick and his deputies arrive.

As I step through the French doors onto the impressive patio, I'm painfully aware of my solitude. Earlier, when I entered the graveyard with the group of cookbook devotees, I felt relaxed and at ease.

Post corpse discovery, I fear there is something lurking behind every bush. Moving toward the steps, I place my hand on the solid concrete wall. A deep breath or two is in order.

Sinking into my extrasensory perceptions, I reach out for anything unusual. The prerecorded ghostly graveyard sounds serve as a disheartening soundtrack for my psychic investigation.

I'm definitely alone in the graveyard. No other living entities are present. The ghost decorations blowing in the trees seem to urge me forward.

Hesitantly, I step toward the painted Styrofoam gravestones and search for footprints beneath the swirling, man-made fog. It's no use. Too many people have tramped through the area. Any signs of a struggle or a distinctive tread pattern have been obscured.

One more step will trigger the coffin. I'm not entirely sure if I want to view the corpse—again—before backup arrives.

As I weigh my decision, the hairs on the back of my neck stand on end. I'm no longer alone. Someone is peering at me. I can feel their gaze on my skin. But from where?

Closing my eyes, I sink deeper and reach out farther. Following the otherworldly sensations, I turn and pop my eyes open. The curtain at a second-floor window quickly closes.

My special abilities offer me no further clue.

Before I can step forward, the patio doors swing wide and Erick strides through, flanked by Deputies Paulsen and Gilbert.

"Where's the body, Moon?"

I wait for him to come closer, and, as he reaches the point of no return, I take that last step. The coffin pops open. "Ta-dah."

To his credit, he neither screams nor jumps.

The same cannot be said for Deputy Paulsen. Not only has she drawn her gun, but she also dropped and rolled behind a Styrofoam gravestone to take up a strategic position.

I point toward the horrid Halloween décor gone wrong. "It's not a prop."

Erick shakes his head, glances down at my foot, and reaches into the display to remove the motion sensor. He tosses it to Gilbert. "Throw that in an evidence bag, in case it matters later." Erick exhales. "And Paulsen, holster your weapon. This one's already dead."

She makes quite a show of checking her weapon before she slips it back into the holster on her hip. "Where are the tour guests, Moon?" She crosses her arms over her chest.

"Since they were all at an event in my bookshop, and were standing behind me when we walked out here, AND Cheryl's body was already in the coffin, I told them to wait in the haunted library. After we called you guys, I sent them on their merry way. However, Mrs. Charles was acting super bajiggity, and Clyde was a hot mess when we got here. He wasn't manning his post, and his vest was—"

Paulsen steps forward, and her right hand quickly slips to the handle of her gun. "This is a matter for the sheriff's department, Moon. You don't make decisions about who gets questioned and who doesn't. We haven't officially established time of death. I'm gonna need a list of everyone who attended that book signing."

Erick steps forward and arches an eyebrow in my general direction before approaching the coffin. "Paulsen, take statements from Mrs. Charles and Clyde. I'll wait here for the coroner."

Paulsen has a solid point about time of death, but Erick didn't openly agree with her and ask me to leave the crime scene. It's easy to see irritation inching across Paulsen's face. "10-4, Sheriff."

Once she leaves the graveyard attraction, I join Erick beside the coffin.

"There wasn't anyone else out here. But someone was watching me from an upstairs window. It was probably Mrs. Charles since she'd hardly let anyone else up there, but it's worth mentioning."

Erick bends toward me and whispers, "Are you getting anything? Is her ghost here?"

I stifle a chuckle and pat him on the shoulder. "Hey, I know you're pretty new to all of this, and I appreciate you're making the effort. Things in the psychic realm don't really happen in a predictable way. I'm not getting any additional information, and, as far as I can tell, Cheryl's ghost is not here. I don't have nearly enough experience to tell you what that means, but I'm just reporting what I see— or don't see."

He crosses his arms in that yummy way that

makes his biceps bulge, and I'm temporarily distracted.

The medical examiner and Deputy Gilbert return and begin processing the crime scene.

Erick and I step back and let them work.

After a cursory examination of the body, the ME turns toward Sheriff Harper. "Cause of death appears to be strangulation, Sheriff. I'll know more when I get her back to my slab. I would say the body was carefully placed, possibly even posed." She turns to Deputy Gilbert. "Can you check the area for any sign of struggle? I'm fairly certain the murder didn't take place in this coffin."

A thought pops into my head, and I squeeze Erick's arm as I tug him out of earshot. "Hey, that could be one reason why I'm not seeing her ghost. If Cheryl's ghost *is* on this side of the veil. If she wasn't killed here, her ghost might be trapped in whatever place the murder happened."

Bless his heart. He nods as though I'm giving him a completely normal weather report. Sheriff Harper walks back to the ME and asks a few additional questions.

She bags some evidence and passes it to the sheriff. "I don't see anything else inside the coffin. But maybe there's a fingerprint on that button."

At the word "button," my ears perk up. "Excuse me, Sheriff. Did she say a button?"

"Yep. Looks like a basic black button approximately one-half-inch to five-eighths of an inch in diameter. Why?"

"Remember how I was saying Clyde was a hot mess when we got here? Well, his vest was buttoned crookedly, but there also may have been a button missing."

Erick nods once, but shakes his head. "I don't know. Clyde is different, but he's not calculating or violent. Plus, he didn't technically know the woman, did he?"

"No, but there was that altercation yesterday. You know how he likes rules and patterns. Cheryl and her assistant got him pretty agitated. Plus, Cheryl said those terrible things and— Well, Mrs. Charles was furious with her."

He drags his left thumb along his jaw, and I can almost see the wheels turning in his head. "True. I'll keep that in mind."

"Oh, gosh! Has anyone told Janet? I don't know if Cheryl has any next of kin, but she seemed rather dependent on her assistant."

Erick nods thoughtfully. "Would you mind giving her a call? It's not exactly protocol, but if you know the woman, it might be better coming from you."

"Me? I don't have her phone number. She made all the arrangements with Twiggy. I think you better leave that to a deputy. Janet and I didn't exactly hit it off."

Erick offers a crooked grin and tilts his head. "So what you're saying is, you don't mind finding the bad news, you just don't want to have to deliver it."

CHAPTER 9

SHERIFF SMARTY-PANTS IS ONLY HALF RIGHT. I
may not want to deliver the information to Janet,
but I certainly can't wait to tell Grams!

After Deputy Gilbert drops me at the bookshop, I ring the bell beside the alleyway door. With
all the hoopla surrounding the book signing and the
soft opening, I didn't bring my key. Luckily, Grams
responds quickly, and she's got enough juice to turn
the handle from the inside.

"You are not going to believe what happened!"

Her ghostly face turns serious, and she presses a
hand to her ample bosom. "You didn't get into a
fight with Erick, did you? It looks like you're all
alone." She exhales with a huff. "If you did something to mess up this pending engagement—"

"Easy, grandmother-of-the-bridezilla. Erick had

to cancel on attending the soft opening, but I found a way to lure him out there."

Grams grins mischievously and floats down to eye level. "See, you learned something from your Gram Gram after all!"

"Oh, don't worry. I think we traced the trollop gene directly back to you quite some time ago."

We share a giggle, and I unzip the itchy zombie bride costume as I hurry toward my apartment. "I'll start by saying we're going to need the murder wall!"

Ghost-ma gasps. "There was a murder? Are you okay? Mitzy! I find it so disappointing when you put yourself in danger."

The bookcase door slides open, and I let the gown fall as I retrieve my reindeer onesie pajamas from the end of the bed. "I wasn't in any danger. The murder was committed before we ever arrived for the tour. In fact, according to the medical examiner, the murder may have been committed somewhere else altogether."

Grams musters all her energy and attempts to move the rolling corkboard that doubles as our murder wall into the middle of the room. "A little help, dear."

"Save your energy for writing up the 3 x 5 cards." I grab the metal frame and roll the board into the middle of the room.

Grabbing her trusty pen, Grams hovers it above the stack of blank cards. "Who's first?"

I can't help but pick the low-hanging fruit. "Did you say who's on first?"

For a split second, she takes me seriously and opens her mouth to explain. However, to her credit, she catches herself and shakes her head wryly. "Whose name am I writing down first?"

"Unfortunately, you'll have to write up a card for Mrs. Charles. I don't want to suspect her, but she was pretty upset with Cheryl earlier this afternoon."

Grams drops her pen and rockets toward the ceiling. "Chiffon Cheryl? Chiffon Cheryl is the victim?"

"Oops. Did I leave that part out?"

She whooshes toward me like an avenging angel. "Yes! You certainly did. I happen to think Chiffon Cheryl is a brilliant baker and obviously has immaculate taste. Did you see what she was wearing the other day? And that was for a casual drop by. I mean, the Valentino shoes alone were to die for. But that fitted Donna Karan blazer—it took my breath away! It has to be the very latest thing. I'd certainly recognize it if it was from a season before I passed."

"Slow down, Anna Wintour. You can stop fangirling over Chiffon Cheryl. She may look good on the outside, but she's rotten to the core. She was absolutely horrid to Clyde, and she got a girl kicked out of cooking school! Did you know she was a classmate of Anne's? Anne said she stole one of her recipes and it's in this cookbook!"

"Oh, my stars! Which recipe?"

At first, the question hardly seems important, but as the images flash through my mind—those from the ring and from my psychic recall—my concern increases. "It was the pin cherry and chocolate chip scone recipe. That was the page—"

"That was the page Mr. Cuddlekins tore from the cookbook! Mitzy . . . you don't think . . ."

"It's not possible, Grams. Anne is one of the kindest people I've ever met. There's no way she murdered Cheryl over a stolen recipe."

Grams folds one arm across her glowing midriff and taps a perfectly manicured finger against her coral lip. "The stolen recipe could just be the tip of the iceberg. I'm afraid we're going to have to write out a card for Anne. What is it you always say? Everyone's a suspect until they aren't."

Pacing across the thick Persian carpet, I can't imagine my favorite pastry chef doing something so out of character. "Fine. Make out a card for Anne. Let the record show, I don't believe for one minute that she had anything to do with this. That being said, you're going to need to write out a card for Clyde as well."

Her features soften, and she shakes her head. "Oh, that dear boy. He adored being on the football team with Erick."

At the mention of the sexy sheriff, Grams has my full attention.

"I thought that might catch your ear." She winks and smirks.

Squeezing my eyelids to narrow slits, I stare at her with simmering rage. "You are not allowed to thought-drop, Myrtle Isadora. No exceptions." I point firmly toward my mouth. "If these lips aren't moving—"

"Oh, for crying out loud, sweetie. Those lips are always moving! You talk in your sleep, and if you're not talking, you're eating! What's a ghost to do?"

I'm not about to let her off the hook that easily. "Heaven forbid a ghost minds her own business."

She relents and writes Clyde's name on a card. I retrieve the completed cards and tack them to the board. Chiffon Cheryl is in the middle, with the suspects on either side.

"Mitzy, what about that mousy assistant?"

"Janet? I don't think so. I did see her having a disagreement with Cheryl. But she was being paid quite well and may have even been blackmailing her employer. Doesn't seem like a very smart move to kill the golden goose."

Ghost-ma exhales dramatically. "Well, I'm writing up a card for her. Let the record show, I'm highly suspicious of assistants."

As I retrieve the card, I can't help myself. "So, should I be opening the case files on Myrtle Isadora? Is Twiggy a suspect?"

Her ghost mouth falls open in utter shock.

"I'm kidding! I know she was your best friend and not an assistant. It was a joke. I swear!"

"Gotcha." Ghost-ma's eyes sparkle with mischief.

"All right, I deserved that." Taking the green yarn and making connections between the victim and the various suspects, no obvious pattern emerges. "I don't know much about Cheryl's life. She could've made all sorts of enemies along the way. Her book signing was heavily publicized. Anyone could've dashed into town, strangled her, and dashed right out again."

Grams reaches for her own throat, and her shimmering fingers stroke across it gently. "Strangulation is personal. Random acquaintances, or a business rival, probably wouldn't risk getting that close to her. Maybe you can look through the packet of publicity information they sent to Twiggy. I think she put it in the built-in desk in the back room."

"Thanks, Grams. Have I told you lately how handy you are to have around?"

She chuckles.

BING. BONG. BING.

"It's late!" Glancing down at my PJs, I decide to risk it.

Grams zips through the wall, and I wait impatiently for the bookcase to slide open.

She's hovering eagerly near the alley door when I finally negotiate the chain and manage to stay on my feet. "Who is it?" I whisper to Grams.

One look at the impish grin on her face, and I have my answer.

Swinging open the door, I place a hand on my curvy hip. "Good evening, Sheriff. Is this business or pleasure?"

He slips his arm around my waist and nuzzles into my neck as he whispers, "I was kinda hoping the *business* would be pleasure."

Suddenly, despite the icy winds knifing across the great lake snuggled in the harbor behind my bookshop, I am instantly overheating.

Grams giggles mercilessly. "I'll see myself to the printing museum, dear. I'm sure you and Erick have a lot to *talk* about." She continues laughing as she phases through the wall.

You're not wrong. I shoot her the telepathic message as she disappears.

"Grams has excused herself, and I don't expect we'll see her till morning. Would you care to come up to my sitting room, Mr. Harper?"

He tips his head in that adorable way that insinuates he's doffing a cap and grins. "Why, I'd be much obliged, Miss Moon."

I giggle and run. He growls and chases.

CHAPTER 10

AN EARLY MORNING call on Erick's cell phone interrupts our Pyewacket-free snuggle time.

"Do you have to answer it?" I tug his arm around me tightly and wiggle closer.

His hot breath on the back of my neck induces a full-body shiver. "Consider yourself saved by the bell, Moon." He throws back the covers, hops out of my antique four-poster bed, and grabs his phone. "Sheriff Harper."

He keeps his voice low, but it's clear he's receiving an update on Chiffon Cheryl's case. You will be so proud of me! I make no "extra" attempt to eavesdrop. Which is to say, I can hear him perfectly without engaging my clairaudience.

He ends the call and shoots me a suspicious look. "Well?"

I paint my features in a portrait of innocence. "You may as well tell me. I heard your side of the conversation, and I have a pretty good idea what was happening on the other end of the call, but I'd love confirmation."

"What do you say we grab breakfast at the diner, and I bring you up to speed?"

I love the touchstone of eating meals in a cozy, homey place. I never thought I'd have something like that in my life. "Deal. Give me five minutes."

He leans back expectantly and hovers a finger above his phone. "On your mark, get set, go!" Erick taps his phone, and experience has taught me the clock is literally ticking. Attempting to hustle out of bed results in a tangled mess of sheets. I manage to stay on my feet, but only by the skin of my teeth.

Splashing cold water on my face, I drag my wet fingers through my haystack of a hairdo and blot the excess drips from my face on a mostly clean hand towel. I already have a solid idea of what I'll be wearing, so I take an extra few seconds to apply a swipe of lip tint and a quick brush of mascara.

Next stop: the mega closet.

I grab my skinny jeans off the floor and hop into them as I search for an appropriate T-shirt. "Pour the coffee, and back away slowly . . ." with a picture of an angry cat, will do nicely. Stumbling out of the closet with my canvas high-tops in my hand, I shout, "Done!"

"Doesn't count unless the shoes are on!" Somehow he's completely dressed and still keeping time.

I clumsily shove my foot in one shoe, but it's the second shoe that does me in. Right foot in the air. Tug. Tug. And crash. Fortunately, I land on a well-padded area, and I'm none the worse for the wear. "Time," I call from the floor.

"You made it just under the wire, Moon."

"You know you're absolutely ridiculous, don't you? I'm a grown woman. I shouldn't have to race against the clock just to have breakfast with my boyfriend."

He scoops an arm around me, hands me my outdoor gear, drags me toward the bookcase door, and presses the twisted ivy medallion. "True. But it's way more fun, right?"

"Touché."

Erick tugs playfully on my scarf as though it were a leash, and I pant after him. I mean, I barely have to pantomime that part!

As we walk into the diner, all heads turn. News of our relationship is yesterday's fish wrap. These guys have all been waiting to eavesdrop on some juicy tidbits about the recent murder. News travels faster than the speed of light in a small town, which is still half a step slower than my favorite waitress—Tally.

We haven't finished sliding across the red-vinyl bench seats, and she's already got coffee and creamer on the table. "Sounds like you had another close call, Mitzy. You sure you're okay?"

You have to give the woman credit. She never asks for gossip outright. "Everything happened before I got there, Tally. I know as much as you do. Probably less."

That brings a chuckle and a ready smile. "Glad to hear you're all in one piece. You know how Odell gets." She nods toward the kitchen and walks to the next table.

I glance past her, expecting the standard spatula salute from my grandfather.

Instead, I see his attention is hyper-focused on the grill in front of him.

Uh oh. That never bodes well.

Moments later, he approaches our table with blueberry pancakes and syrup for Erick and my standard scrambled eggs with chorizo, home fries, and—I swear to you—the same bottle of Tabasco sauce I've been working on since I came to town!

"You're not gonna be happy until you get yourself killed." His expression is more concern than disappointment.

"I'll tell you the same thing I told Isadora."

At the mention of my grandmother's ghost, he gulps, and his eyes dart left and right. "Keep that under your hat, kid."

Crossing my arms, I smile and gaze up at my overprotective grandfather. "I was never in any danger. The crime took place before I arrived on the scene. Erick is about to give me an update. Would you care to join us?"

He sniffs sharply. "I got a diner to run." He raps his knuckles twice on the silver-flecked Formica table and returns to his cookery duties.

Erick slathers his stack with pure Canadian maple syrup and shakes his head. "I'd appreciate it if you'd stop announcing to the world that I share confidential information with you."

"Of course. I mean, everyone assumes it anyway. But if you'd rather I didn't advertise, I'll do my best."

His shoulders sag in defeat, and he digs into his luscious breakfast.

I shake Tabasco liberally over my home fries, and a small squeal escapes when the drops cease. My eyes dart to the kitchen, only to be met with the sparkle in my grandfather's deep-brown peepers. His hand disappears below the orders-up window, and when it returns into view, he's tilting an unopened bottle of Tabasco back and forth.

Nodding humbly, I offer him a salute. He always knows what his locals need. Even before they do. How dare I doubt his prowess!

Digging into my breakfast, I gesture for Erick to begin the information download.

"The ME said it was pretty cut and dried. The attacker strangled Cheryl from behind. There were no defensive wounds and nothing significant under her fingernails. If she fought back, her attacker was likely in a thick coat and gloves—or otherwise protected. There are a few more tests to run for particulate, and, later today, those results will conclusively identify the fiber she recovered. The bad news is there was a fingerprint on the button. It was Clyde's."

I immediately stop chewing and swallow with difficulty. "Anyone else's? Maybe it was planted. Was she sure there weren't any other prints? Even a partial?"

He takes a steadying sip of his java and shakes his head. "Nope. Just Clyde's. Paulsen headed out there this morning to ask him some follow-up questions."

"I should drive—"

"What's that? You have business at the Barnes estate? Okay, Moon. But I don't want you interfering with our investigation. Got it?"

"Copy that, Sheriff." My over-the-top wink is unnecessary, but appreciated.

Erick exhales and finishes his coffee. "I better head into the office." He slides out of the booth and pauses. "Hey, your haunted house will have to remain closed until we finish the investigation. I'm sorry, but I can't make an exception. It's an active crime scene."

My initial instinct is to argue and beg a favor, but luckily Isadora's constant lectures about getting more flies with honey are finally sinking in. I nod and smile. "Understood. I'll get to work on finding the actual crime scene, and that should wrap up the nonsense at the Barnes estate."

Sheriff Harper rises to his full six feet and change. "Do not put yourself in danger. And do not tamper with evidence. Are we clear?"

"As mud, Sheriff."

He blows a raspberry through his pouty lips, hangs his head, and exits the diner.

Yes, I lean out of the booth and watch him walk away. I mean, it's not to be missed.

ON THE DRIVE OUT TO THE BARNES ESTATE, I review Erick's exact words. He specifically told me not to put myself in danger and not to tamper with any evidence. In my opinion, that leaves the rest of the Barnes estate—and the employees—wide open.

Since it's not my first *intrusion* at the imposing

mansion, I pull around back and let myself in through the employee entrance. I worked under-cover as a faux British maid here for a hot minute. But that's another story.

There's no sign of Paulsen. Sigh of relief.

The massive manor is quiet. Possibly too quiet. Reaching out with my extrasensory perception, I search for signs of life. Without any clues from the great beyond, I head straight for the garden, which currently serves as the haunted graveyard.

My shoulders are pinched together from the tension. Hopefully, I don't end up with a crick in my neck. The constant fear that Mrs. Charles will zoom around the corner and light into me is defi-nitely interfering with my abilities. When I open the French doors onto the granite patio, shock knifes through my chest.

Clyde is busy digging a hole in the garden.

Neither my moody mood ring nor my psychic senses gave me any warning.

A quick glance left, right, and all around reveals no sign of the stern matron. This may be my only chance to question Clyde without his mother present.

Donning a friendly smile and what I hope is a casual air, I approach. "Good morning, Clyde. What are you planting?"

Guilt grips his features. He drops the shovel full

of dirt directly into the hole. He stomps it down and attempts to hide the shovel behind his back.

"Clyde, is everything all right?"

He nods immediately, but his wide eyes and tightly pressed lips would indicate otherwise.

"I hope you know you can trust me. I might be dating the sheriff, but I'm on the side of protecting the innocent. I'm not here to point the finger at anyone. You can talk to me. It's safe."

He swallows with difficulty and shakes his head. "Mom— Mrs. Charles said not to speak to anyone."

"You gave a statement to Deputy Paulsen. Didn't you?"

Clearly, this question stumps him. His eyes dart in his head and he nods slowly. "I did."

"That's great. You can tell me what you told her. Technically, it's already public record. You know anything you say in conjunction with an investigation is in the police report, right? I can get a copy. I just thought it would be nice if we chatted. We are friends, aren't we?"

He nods fervently. "Yes. You're a good friend, Miss Moon."

"Thank you, Clyde. I feel the same way about you." I take a step closer, hoping to see evidence of whatever he was burying in the hole. Because the longer I stand here, the more I realize he wasn't digging a hole. He was filling one in. "So, what did you tell Deputy Paulsen?"

"I told her my name, Clyde Woodruff Charles. I told her my age, thirty-three."

Oh, brother. It's gonna take a while to get to the juicy tidbits.

Clyde continues. "I told her my address, 17—"

"Excuse me, Clyde. I appreciate your attention to detail. But you can skip ahead to when you told her about—you know—what we found in the coffin."

His Adam's apple struggles mightily, and he finally swallows. A quick glance toward the coffin results in a pink flush on his cheeks. "I didn't tell her about that."

"What do you mean? I thought you said you gave your statement to Deputy Paulsen. You did, didn't you?"

"I told her all the stuff I was telling you. Then mother, Mrs. Charles, told me I didn't have to say anything else. Without a lawyer."

"What? Why would Mrs. Charles say without a lawyer? Clyde, are you in trouble? I can help you. I have a lawyer. Mr. Willoughby would be happy to represent you. But why would you need a lawyer if you're innocent?" My mind is spinning faster than my mouth. I pause and gather my wits. "You better tell me what happened. This sounds very serious. I have a lot of experience with legal matters. I promise you can trust me, Clyde."

His eyes scan the vista for any sign of his mother. Finding none, he weakens at last. "I was making a final check of the house and grounds. I like to make sure everything is in order before I open the door. If something is out of place or a light isn't turned on, it can ruin a visitor's experience. I like things to be just right."

"I know you do, Clyde. And I've always appreciated that. So, what happened on your final check?"

"When I opened the French doors, they bumped into—" His eyes tear up, and the sight breaks my heart.

"You don't have to say it, Clyde. I know what you're talking about. You found Cheryl. Was she alive?"

He drops the shovel that he'd been holding behind his back and grips his hands tightly in front of himself. His knuckles whiten as he squeezes the flesh of his large hands. "I don't know. I got mother right away. I didn't know what to do. I've never— It wasn't on my list."

"I understand. That was the right thing to do. What did your mother say when she came back to Cheryl's body?"

"She was very upset with me. She said, 'big mistake.' Or maybe she said, 'big milkshake.' I don't remember. I was very agitated. I couldn't breathe very good."

"It's all right. Take a deep breath right now. Did she tell you to call the police?"

Clyde shakes his head. "No. She kept saying this won't do. This won't do. And then she told me to help her."

"To help her how? Was she injured?"

"No, she had on her Sunday wool coat and leather gloves. She had been outside lighting the pumpkins. It was cold."

Something the medical examiner said is tickling the back of my skull. "What happened next, Clyde?"

"I helped her put the—you know—in the coffin. And I put the prop skeleton out in the garden shed like she told me. She said the lady was pretending, and that it was a game." He draws a shaky breath. "But Deputy Paulsen used the word *murder*."

"Oh, Clyde. I'm so sorry. Thank you for telling me." I reach out to pat him on the shoulder, and he flinches. "I'm sorry, Clyde. I was only trying to comfort you. I would never hurt you."

He nods, but the expression on his face tells a different story. He has been hurt. His trust doesn't come easy.

Best to change tactics. "Do you remember your

mother getting dirt on her face when you placed Cheryl in the Halloween coffin?"

Clyde becomes very still. It's difficult to discern whether he's trying to remember, or trying to create a lie. "I didn't see any dirt."

"All right. Thank you for talk—"

"What on earth is going on here? You have no business speaking to my son when I'm not present."

Holy *Mr. Deeds*! She's sneakier than that butler, Emilio. I throw all burners on full whack and cook up my story. "Mrs. Charles! It's great to see you. I came out to tell you and Clyde the haunted mansion attraction will be closed until the sheriff finishes the investigation. I looked for you in the house first, and when I stepped into the garden, I happened upon Clyde."

Her eyes narrow to judgmental slits, and it's clear that she has no intention of buying my story. "That hardly required a trip out to the manor, Miss Moon. A simple phone call would have sufficed."

"Of course. But I was worried about the two of you." Stepping toward her and lowering my voice, I whisper, "Someone was murdered on the grounds. The police have no leads. You both could be in danger. Would you like me to put you up at a hotel in town?"

This approach seems to throw her temporarily

off the scent. "Pshaw. Clyde and I can take care of ourselves. I appreciate your concern."

Reaching toward her arm to offer a comforting pat, she flinches in the same manner as her son. Hmmm. I'll be making a note of that.

"Well, I best be getting back to town. I wanted you to know that the Duncan-Moon Foundation will continue to pay the agreed-upon rental charges for the full duration of the contract, even though we're not able to have guests at this time. Hopefully, Sheriff Harper will wrap this up quickly, and we'll at least be able to conduct tours during the Halloween weekend."

Mrs. Charles exhales in frustration, or perhaps relief, and smooths her dress. "Clyde will walk you to your car."

"Oh, that's not necessary. I parked around back. Is there an exit through the garden?"

Her jaw muscles tense, and her lips press together. A fine white line forms above her top lip and her left eyebrow twitches. "Yes. Stay to the right, and you'll find a gate between the weeping willows. It leads into the *employee* parking area."

Mrs. Charles' overemphasis of the word employee brings a smile to my lips. "Thanks. Seems like a lovely day for a walk."

CHAPTER 11

THE ONCE LUSH GARDENS are sorely lacking in the crisp pre-winter air. Verdant evergreen hedges still hold their carefully trimmed shapes, but there is an overall absence of color and warmth.

When I near the bare branches of the weeping willows, a strange memory tickles the back of my mind. There were two large weeping willows—Where? Was it outside an apartment? No. My mother and I lived in a very cramped neighborhood. No room for large trees or lush foliage. Am I—?

Before I can answer my own question, a vision hits me with such force I fall to my knees on the crushed-gravel path.

I'm running. I don't feel fear, but adrenaline is coursing through my veins. My toe catches. I trip and fall, but my thick gloves protect my hands.

Struggling to get my feet beneath me, I lunge for the gate, yank it open, and race through.

Everything fades to black.

The vision ends, and my stomach churns.

Whoa! That's new!

Getting to my feet, I stumble to the Jeep, hop inside, and lock the doors. I'm only guessing, but I think what I experienced was a vision or memory from the killer's perspective.

Maybe it happened because I was walking the same path, or— I have no idea.

I need to get back to the bookshop and call Silas. We have an unofficial agreement about reporting new powers, or abilities, when they surface.

The drive into town temporarily distracts me. As soon as I pull the Jeep into the garage and step into the bookshop, the full impact of my experience hits me like a brick wall. I open my mouth to call out for Grams, but the urgent ringing of my cell phone takes precedence.

It's Erick.

Placing the call on speaker, I step into the back room. "You're not gonna believe what just happened."

"Hey, I called you, remember?" Erick chuckles.

"Oh, right? What's up?"

"Guess who just called me?"

With zero effort on my part, a name pops into

my head. Silas refers to this as my claircognizance—just knowing things. "Eddie?"

Erick exhales as though someone has punched him in the gut. "How do you—? Never mind. I should've known better than to ask you to guess. But you're right, Eddie, the TSA agent at the airport, caught Janet making a break for it."

"What? Janet? Why?"

Erick gives a low whistle. "Paulsen said Janet was noticeably unemotional when she learned of Cheryl's death. Of course, Paulsen told her not to leave town, but the next thing you know, she's at the airport!"

"But how did Eddie know? Did you put out a BOLO or some . . .? I mean, he's—"

"Let me help you out, Moon. Eddie is extremely observant. He said he noted the pair when they flew into town, and he, like all residents of Pin Cherry Harbor, had heard about Cheryl's untimely death. Eddie and I go way back, so when he saw Janet leaving so soon after the murder, he was suspicious. He figured better safe than sorry and gave me a call. I can tell you, Janet was none too happy to be caught in the act of fleeing."

"But why would she flee? Are you saying she's a legitimate suspect?"

"Legitimate? As far as I'm concerned, she's my

only suspect. No one else in town even knew Cheryl."

"What about Anne?" Shoot! As soon as the words escape from my mouth, I feel nothing but regret.

"What do you mean?"

Shoot. Shoot. Shoot. "I'm sure it's nothing. Anne and Cheryl went to culinary school together. Pure coincidence."

He exhales. "What *aren't* you telling me, Moon?"

"Well, Pyewacket tore a page out of Cheryl's cookbook. It was Anne's scone recipe. Apparently, Cheryl stole the recipe from her when they were in school and published it without permission. But, come on, we both know Anne would never—"

"Hey, I'm on your side, but I have to follow every lead. Janet's in holding. I'll stop by and talk to Anne, just as a formality. Now, what's going on with you?"

News of Janet's attempted cut and run almost made me lose my focus. "I headed out to the Barnes place and talked to Clyde."

"Mitzy, I told you not to meddle in this case."

"False. You told me not to put myself in danger, and you told me not to tamper with evidence. And, to be clear, I didn't tamper with any evidence. However, I would love it if you'd accompany me back to the mansion this evening when I sneak out there to dig up whatever Clyde was burying."

"Under no circumstances are you going to trespass at the Barnes mansion and abscond with potential evidence."

"It's my lead, Sheriff."

"For the hundredth time, Mitzy, you're not a cop. You're not even a private investigator. You're just a snoopy—"

"Hold on, boss. I believe one of Pin Cherry Harbor's finest dubbed me an honorary deputy. I can't be certain, but I'm pretty sure that comes with a few benefits. Are you coming with me tonight or not?"

There's a long silence, and I can feel his frustration oozing through the phone. "Great. Obviously, I have no idea where to look for this buried object. But I'll make sure we have a warrant and an evidence bag. This is gonna be handled professionally. No amateur stuff. Got it?"

"Copy that." My snicker escapes unbidden. "By the way, Clyde said he didn't give a statement to Paulsen. I mean, he gave his particulars, but Mrs. Charles shut it down before he told his whole story."

Erick groans in agreement. "That's right. Mrs. Charles said we couldn't question him without a lawyer present. As you know, Paulsen thinks that anyone who has to lawyer up is guilty by default."

I take a dramatic beat. "He didn't need a lawyer when he talked to me."

Soft chuckles bubble from the speaker. "Are you planning on sharing the rest of the story?"

"Now that you've agreed to accompany me on my midnight dig, I'll tell you anything you want to know, Sheriff Harper."

It suddenly occurs to me that if I share Clyde's story, Erick's justice meter will spike off the charts. He'll immediately race out to the manor and bring him in. I have absolutely no evidence to support my theory, but something tells me Clyde is innocent. Time to rearrange the order of my playing cards. "I tell you what, Sheriff. How about you handle this Janet interview, I wait patiently in your office, and we discuss Clyde's story on our way out to recover the buried item? It's not that I don't trust you, Harper. But I don't want to play my trump card too soon."

His labored exhale is laden with frustration. "Have you ever actually played cards, Moon?"

"Well, there was that one time I played blackjack—"

"Forget it. It's no use arguing with you. Come on over to the station, and you can hang out in my office while I do the paperwork for that warrant. It might be handy for you to see that not all police work is kicking down doors and engaging in shootouts with perps."

Laughter grips me. "I'll see you shortly. I'm not giving an exact time, because I'm not playing *Beat the Clock!*"

His laughter is the last thing I hear as he ends the call.

Once we recover the buried item, I'll update the murder wall and see if my mood ring or my fiendish feline feels like sharing any additional information.

Furious Monkeys is enthralled by her smartphone and can barely be bothered to offer me a brief head nod toward the sheriff's office.

The scarred wooden gate squeaks closed behind me, and the bullpen is empty. Must be a busy crime day in old Pin Cherry.

Erick looks up as I walk in and can't keep the smile from his face, even though he's mildly irritated with me. "Have a seat, Moon. You're about to see the magic of paperwork."

"Hilarious." I plunk myself onto one of the uncomfortable guest chairs and fiddle with my shoelaces as Erick fills out his precious form. Boredom is sucking the life from my very soul. Leaning forward, I stare at his penmanship. "You know what? I don't think I ever really noticed how neatly you print. Is that genetic, or do you have a worksheet you practice on at home?" I can only keep the smile from my face for a couple of seconds, but it's long enough for him to look up and scowl.

"Easy, Sheriff. It was a joke. I'm trying to lighten the mood."

He drops his pen, leans back, and laces his fingers behind his head as he sighs.

Old habits die hard, and my eyes dart toward his hidden washboard abs. Too bad that gosh darn uniform shirt is tucked in so tightly. No sneak peek today.

He tilts a bit farther in his chair, and the groaning of the ancient springs concerns me. Erick doesn't seem to notice the troublesome noise. "Mitzy, I might be getting the cart ahead of the horse here, but we need to talk."

My right ankle slips off my left knee, and any remaining life force drains from me. Nothing good ever comes after those four little words.

He leans forward and fidgets with his pen. "You know I love you, right?"

Oh, boy! It's definitely getting worse. "Yes."

"And you know I admire your abilities, or whatever you call them."

Wow! This is headed directly down the toilet. "All right."

"But if we were to get married, you'd have to stop. You understand, don't you?"

The room feels as though it's spinning, and I press my hands to the sides of my head to try to stave off the dizziness. "Stop what? What exactly are you saying, Erick?"

He rolls the pencil roughly between his fingers, and it snaps in half. His eyes widen and he swallows with effort. "Well, it's one thing for my girlfriend to be poking around in cases and eavesdropping on suspect interviews, but—"

"But what?" I plant my feet firmly on the floor, and the dizziness vanishes. I don't like where this is headed, and I'm about to stand up and tell him so.

"It's just that if— Oh, this isn't coming out right. As my wife, it's a whole different story. It crosses a line. There could be serious repercussions. For you, for me, for the whole department. I'm sure there's something else you could do. You have other skills, right?"

The need to storm out dramatically and the need to eavesdrop on an important suspect interview are battling a cage match in my head. "I hear what you're saying. However, if we're going to have this talk, then perhaps you should consider doing something else. You also have other skills, right?"

His deep-blue eyes cloud over. It clearly never occurred to him that I would lob the career-change volley back into his court.

"I'm the sheriff. I'm responsible for protecting an entire county. You're—"

That's it. I jolt to my feet and give him the "stop in the name of love" hand. "For your own safety, and the future of our relationship, do not finish that sentence. I'm going to get a drink of water, and I think you have a suspect to question. We'll table this discussion."

He stands, hangs his head, and shuffles toward me. "I love everything about you, Mitzy. You're the best thing that ever happened to me. Heck, you're probably the best thing that ever happened to this whole town. I definitely don't want to lose you, but we have to talk about this. Not necessarily today. But at some point."

Erick's nearness interferes with my ability to stay angry. His citrus-woodsy scent seems to hypnotize me. I snuggle into the firm planes of his chest. "Fine. Truce. Once we solve this case—"

He whispers softly, "And finish the séance."

Tilting my head up, I kiss his soft, full lips. "Yeah. After all of that, you and I are gonna have a big old grown-up discussion. Pinky promise?"

He slides his long sexy fingers up my arm and hooks his pinky through mine. "Pinky promise."

CHAPTER 12

ERICK HEADS TO LOCK-UP to retrieve Janet, while I sit and pretend to wait patiently in his office. A lone typewriter taps out a rhythm in the bullpen, and air flutters through a vent above my head. It's not particularly warm, and it carries the fine dust of ages past as it filters into the small space. Footsteps in the hallway grab my attention.

Once he escorts her into Interrogation Room Two, I glance up and down the hallway and dart into the observation room sandwiched between the two interview spaces. I flip the toggle by the speaker and sit back. The lovely shape of the back of Erick's head could distract me for hours . . .

Focus, Moon!

He exhales and offers a friendly nod. "Miss

Ferro, I picked you up at the airport today. Do you know why?"

She stares at the hands folded in her lap and replies, "Because the TSA agent called you."

Erick tilts his head, and, even from behind, I can see the muscles in his jaw clench. "Yes. Do you know why he called me?"

"No. He asked me to wait in the office. He stepped outside to call you. I couldn't hear what was said."

The sheriff rolls his shoulders back. "You were told not to leave town, Miss Ferro. Deputy Paulsen gave you explicit instructions to remain here until the investigation was closed. The TSA agent called me because you attempted to flee the area."

Her eyelids squeeze together ever so slightly. "No. I had a ticket. My flight left at eleven o'clock today. I had a ticket."

"But our investigation wasn't complete, Miss Ferro. You should have gotten another ticket after the investigation was closed."

Janet shakes her head vigorously. "There would have been charges for changing the ticket. Cheryl was very particular about expenses. I'm to keep my expenses to a minimum. She has to approve any overages. She wasn't available to approve an overage."

Wisely, Erick abandons this line of questioning and delves into his standard rundown.

Also worth noting, Janet easily spoke of Cheryl in the past tense. She didn't stumble or stutter and awkwardly switch from present to past. She came right out of the gate with "was."

Janet gives Sheriff Harper her details while her hands remain folded in her lap. She appears calm and disinterested.

I sink into my extrasensory perceptions and use the technique Silas taught me about visualizing myself as a catcher's mitt. Rather than attempting to probe into Janet's psyche, I hold a space for the information to come to me.

Nothing. Nada. Bupkus.

Her exterior and interior feel as though they are in perfect sync.

Weird. Even if she were innocent, most people would get mildly agitated around law-enforcement officials.

Erick proceeds with his basic questions regarding her whereabouts, her movements leading up to the time of death window, and her reasons for taking Cheryl out to the Barnes estate a second time, despite the warning about trespassing.

Janet is impenetrable. In the calmest voice I've ever heard, she answers each of Erick's questions succinctly.

"Cheryl is a big fan of Halloween. She didn't want to impose on Miss Moon, and she didn't wish to view the haunted attraction with a large group. She asked me to take her out earlier in the day so that she could have a private experience. The doorman was quite hostile toward us and, once again, refused to let us enter."

Erick nods. "Did you call ahead?"

Janet shakes her head. "Cheryl is a celebrity pastry chef. She's not accustomed to calling ahead for anything. Generally, her star power is enough to bend any rule that stands in her way."

There's a hint of irritation building in Janet's voice, but nothing alarming.

"And then what happened?" Sheriff Harper makes a note in his pad.

Janet relays the events that led up to another confrontation with Mrs. Charles, but she doesn't shed any light on the events that followed.

"Once Cheryl convinced Mrs. Charles to allow her to tour the haunted house, I went back to the hotel. There were literally hundreds of emails that needed to be handled and several details of the book tour that had to be finalized. Pin Cherry Harbor was only the first stop on a multi-city tour."

She finally gives off enough energy for me to get a sliver of info. Exasperation, frustration, and possibly genuine exhaustion. But guilt? Not a whiff.

Erick nods. "And when did you return to pick Cheryl up from the haunted house attraction?"

"I didn't. She has the direct number for the local car service. I assumed she would call them when she was ready to return to the hotel."

"Were you concerned when she didn't return?"

"No. Cheryl is an independent woman. She's not shy about telling people what she needs. If she had required something from me, she would have called."

Sheriff Harper adjusts himself in the chair, and silence hangs between them.

I can definitely sense his frustration. There were no holes in Janet's story. He didn't trip her up, and he hasn't gained any useful information.

"What about when she didn't show up for the book signing? Did that concern you?"

Janet sits silently for a moment, and I'm wondering whether she'll ever answer the question.

Eventually, she inhales and responds. "I was concerned about bad publicity. It never occurred to me to be concerned for Cheryl's safety. I had no reason to suspect anything was wrong."

Erick outwardly keeps his cool, but I sense his patience waning. "You don't seem particularly upset about your employer's death, Miss Ferro."

Janet stares silently and blinks several times. "I will have to look for other employment. Chiffon

Cheryl and I were not friends. She was my boss, and I did my job to the best of my abilities. Certainly, it is upsetting when someone dies, but she and I were not friends."

The mood ring on my left hand springs to life—at last. An icy chill encircles my finger, and I glance down to see an image of Clyde. At first, the clue makes little sense. However, once the word *Asperger's* bubbles to the surface, the pieces fall into place like a Rubik's cube.

I've been warned about interfering, but this information is incredibly important.

Hopping out of the chair, I knock urgently on the one-way glass.

Erick stiffens, and I feel his anger nearing the boil.

No point racing back to his office to play make-believe. I'll stay put and hope my newsflash is enough to cool his percolating rage.

The door opens forcefully, and Erick marches in. "Mitzy, what were we just talking about?"

"She has Asperger's. Or she's on the spectrum. That's why it's hard to read her emotions and might be why she's reacting in an unusual way to Cheryl's death. I thought you should know. It might help you with the interview."

His anger evaporates, and he smiles. A hint of pride ripples across his face. "Okay. You win. That's extremely helpful information, and not something I would've thought to ask. Thank you."

Grabbing the edge of my T-shirt, I pull it out and feign a curtsy. "Helpful citizen, Mitzy Moon, at your service, Sheriff."

He rolls his eyes, chuckles, and returns to the interrogation room.

Scraping my chair closer to the speaker, I eagerly await the rest of the interview.

"Do you need a glass of water, Miss Ferro?"

Janet glances up briefly, blinks, and shakes her head. "I'm not thirsty."

Erick takes his seat—and a deep breath. "Miss Ferro, may I ask a personal question?"

She nods.

"Have you ever been diagnosed with Asperger's or been told that you are on the autism spectrum?"

Rather than shock, her expression softens and her eyes brighten. "Yes."

You've got to hand it to Janet. She does not mince words.

She adjusts the green scarf decoratively looped around her neck and pinned with a silver brooch, and places her hands back in her lap.

"Well, Miss Ferro, we'll speak to the hotel staff to confirm your alibi. If we're able to confirm your movements, you'll be released. If you're released, I must insist that you not leave Pin Cherry Harbor until this investigation is closed, even if that means purchasing a new ticket causing an unapproved overage. Do you understand?"

Once Erick secures agreement from Janet, he takes her back to lock-up.

I flick the switch to turn off the speaker and return to Erick's office.

After he returns Janet to her cell, he flops onto his ancient office chair like a scolded dog. "What a mess."

"Don't worry. We'll figure it out. We always figure them out."

He creaks backward and shakes his head. "She was my best suspect. I thought her attempt to flee was an admission of guilt. After that interview, I know less than I knew before. Is someone like that even capable of planning a murder?"

Leaning forward, I place my elbows on his desk and attempt to use my feminine wiles to lift his spirits. "Hey, don't lose faith." Bat, bat, bat of the eyelashes. "Janet is clearly intelligent. She manages Cheryl's entire schedule, and, as near as I can tell, practically writes the books!" Sultry smile. Wink. "Someone with a skill set like that could plan anything."

Erick scrunches up his mouth with a sliver of hope. "So you think she might be guilty?"

With a defeated exhale, I press my back against

the uncomfortable visitor's chair. "Unfortunately, I can't get a read off of her. Other than the hit about her being on the spectrum, I couldn't tell if she was speaking the truth or not. She doesn't seem to be super in touch with her emotions. Usually, that's what gives someone away. With her, I get nothing."

He rubs his hands across his face and nods slowly. "Same. I can usually tell if somebody's guilty or innocent after the first four or five questions. With her, every question I asked just left me more confused. I'll have Johnson check her alibi, and—"

The mic clipped to his shoulder sounds off. "The ME needs a call, Sheriff."

He depresses the button. "10-4." Erick glances at me, probably thinks about asking me to leave, but abandons that idea and calls the medical examiner. "Sheriff Harper here. Got an update?"

I lean forward in an attempt to eavesdrop, but the person on the other end of the phone must be a low-talker. No dice.

Erick hangs up the phone and smiles. "She's identified the fiber. It's one hundred percent pure silk. Some specific shade of orange with flecks of black and gold. I think she said the main color was burnt sienna. Anyway, it will be in the report. Apparently, it's a high-quality grade of silk that's used in designer scarves."

"Janet was wearing a scarf that color when I saw her and Cheryl at the patisserie. But today her scarf was mostly green."

He shrugs. "Based on the ligature marks on the victim's neck, it's a safe bet the scarf was used as the murder weapon and that's why a fiber was left behind. I'll get a warrant to search her suitcases and see if that orange scarf is among her clothing items."

"Great. Do you wanna grab some lunch?"

He tilts his head suddenly. "The queen of leftfield."

"People eat, Erick. It wasn't that obscure."

"I'll have to make some progress on this investigation before I have an appetite."

I scoff openly at his lack of appetite and head for the door. "Sorry to say I can't relate, Sheriff." Gripping the edge of the doorframe, I lean backward and whisper. "See you tonight for our adventure."

Erick chuckles and shakes his head.

Time to get my rig rollin' and refuel so I can update the murder wall. Plus, Grams will be furious to learn that a piece of clothing was used as a murder weapon!

CHAPTER 13

WHEN I APPROACH the bookshop on the corner of First Avenue and Main Street, I grab the handle on the ornately carved front door and pause. Life seems to chug along at quite a clip, and most days I don't bother to stop and admire this beautiful piece of artwork that serves as the entrance to my store.

Today, I pause and smile as my eyes drift over the thick wooden door, intricately carved with whimsical vignettes, such as: a centaur chasing a maiden through delicate woodland; a faun playing a flute for a family of rabbits dancing around his cloven feet; the shadow of a winged horse passing in front of the moon; a wildcat stalking a small boy—a cat who bears a striking resemblance to Pyewacket.

After giving the beautiful piece its due, I pull the handle. The door does not budge.

Weird. It's technically during business hours.

A quick glance to my left reveals Twiggy's well-worn sign taped in the window. "Closed for Collection Trip." In classic Twiggy fashion, there are no details regarding when she will return or when the bookshop will reopen. Fortunately, my grandmother left me a healthy inheritance, and I'm not required to rely on book sales to fund my mediocre lifestyle.

Not mediocre in the sense that I don't enjoy it. Merely in the sense that it's pretty ordinary most days. I'm not prone to extravagance. Unlike my predecessor, Myrtle Isadora!

Of course, the reason I have no need to purchase luxury items is that she pre-purchased everything a girl like me could ever dream of needing. She must have had some pretty darn accurate premonitions about me before she crossed over.

I pull out the triangular-barreled brass key dangling on the chain beneath my T-shirt and feel its heft in my hand. Sliding the key into the lock, I twist it three times and bask in the harmonious sensation that courses through my fingers toward my heart.

There is something symbiotic between this bookstore and me. Maybe it's the energy of my grandmother's ghost that somehow lives within the walls, or maybe it's something even more supernatural that I have yet to discover. Either way, it's comforting and welcoming.

Since we seem to be closed, I secure the door behind myself.

Sensing another presence in the bookshop, I creep up the circular stairs and peer into the Rare Books Loft. Nothing could have prepared me for the tableau.

"What in the *Shadowhunters* is going on?" The oak reading tables and brass lamps, with their delicate green-glass shades, have all been moved into the narrow curving arms of the mezzanine. In the main area, where the tables usually reside, the thick Persian carpets have been carefully rolled back to reveal a dark hardwood floor with an enormous pentacle carved into its surface.

Silas finishes rolling the final carpet, stands, and dusts off his hands as though he's simply planted a row of potatoes. "Ah, at last. We have much to discuss."

"Ya think? What exactly am I looking at, Silas?"

"The large symbol is a pentacle. There are several groupings of alchemical symbols within the larger pattern. Each grouping signifies a specific desired outcome, and—"

"Silas! Has this been under my carpet the entire time? What the heck is going on?"

He harrumphs and smooths his bushy grey

mustache. "I believe your question pertains more to the origin of the carving on this particular floor, rather than an overarching quest for knowledge in symbology or alchemy. Is that correct, Mizithra?"

Ignoring the possibility of an impending lesson, I forge ahead. "Yes. I'm asking you why on earth there is a giant Satan symbol on my floor!"

"You are sadly misinformed—as are most. The pentacle has no connection whatsoever to the being commonly referred to as Satan or the devil. The pentacle is ultimately a symbol that predates organized religion. It is the melding of elements, energies, and influences. Originally, it was used as a sigil of protection, with each point of the star representing a sense to be protected. Sight. Sound. Hearing. Touch. Taste. The encompassing circle held all these concepts in harmony. Symbols are imbued with power by the intentions of those who wield them. This particular grouping was created for your grandmother's benefit."

Regardless of my dislike for lessons, he has my rapt attention. "Why?"

"In order to prepare her spirit for the trials and tribulations of being tethered to this bookshop, we were required to perform a number of intricate ceremonies. Creating a permanent ritual space facilitated a reliable schedule."

I shake my head and shrug. "Leave it to you to

make it sound as though you and Grams were setting up a weekly book club."

He exhales slowly and shakes his head. "By no means. The work your grandmother and I performed proved delicate, tedious, and entirely unproven. Until—"

"Until she died." Even though her ghost resides in my bookshop, the thought of her physical death brings tears to my eyes. "Did she suffer?"

"Physically or spiritually?" he inquires.

"Both."

"I have never lied to you, Mizithra. I must answer yes. The illness that took your grandmother was filled with bouts of darkness. She has always been a strong, determined woman. Despite the pain and physical limitations that crippled her near the end, she pushed on. She endured. It is my belief that she survived by will alone until the last ceremony was complete."

Now I'm bawling like a baby. "I need a tissue." I skirt around the outer curvature of the pentacle and retrieve a box of tissues from my apartment. While I dab at my tears and blow my nose, Silas continues. "It was an arduous task to steel her spirit against the pull."

"The pull?" I sit cross-legged on the floor and hang on his every word.

"When the physical body ceases to live, the

spirit is pulled inexorably toward what is beyond the veil. In order to tether Isadora to this place, we had to ensure that she could resist that pull. Now, there are certain circumstances where an accident or kismet traps a spirit on this side of the veil—as you well know. But, as we've discussed, this frequently results in either a severe melancholy or a dangerous rage. Either can happen in the blink of an eye, or it may take eons, but a spirit that is prevented from completing its posthumous journey can become dangerous."

"Like Mrs. Schloss?" Hopefully, he knows I'm referring to the Fox Mountain ghost. I don't want to revisit that story!

"Precisely. Isadora and I endeavored to prevent that outcome. We intended to tether her spirit on this side of the veil, remove the ache of the pull, and allow her a joyous existence in the realm of the living."

My heart swells in my chest as I relive the many joyous moments I've shared with her. "You did it! Somehow, you and Grams really pulled it off. Do you think anyone else has accomplished this?"

Silas twitches his mustache thoughtfully. "It is not something one discusses. I am not so bold as to imagine I am the only living soul to have placed the pieces of this puzzle in the proper order. However, it is a convoluted process and requires a strength of spirit few possess."

"You mean Isadora's spirit?"

"Indeed."

"So, why are you uncovering this now? Do you have to perform another ceremony for Grams?"

He inhales sharply and shakes his head. "No, Mizithra. This is for you."

Gulp. "Me?"

"I have completed my research regarding the séance. Conducting our conversation with your mother within the boundaries of this sacred space will provide the best protection I can deduce. Are you certain you wish to proceed?"

My heart screams yes, but as my eyes scan over the intricately carved symbols, my stomach churns. "I want to talk to her so badly. But now that Erick is involved, I'm worried about him. He's not like you and me, Silas. What if something happens to him?"

Silas exhales loudly. "It is so like you to misplace your concern. Erick's naïveté is precisely the thing that will protect him. It is you, Mizithra Achelois Moon, who should be worried. You possess a rare combination of psychic gifts and alchemical abilities. For a restless spirit seeking a channel into this world, you would be considered quite a catch."

Normally, a compliment like that would bring a smile to my face. Instead, a frightening chill swirls around me, leaving my skin covered in goosebumps. "But this starry circle business on the floor will keep me safe?"

"This pentacle and the alchemical symbols that support it will provide the best protection possible. However, when dealing with the spirit world, there is no such thing as a foolproof plan. You are assuming a great deal of risk."

"Understood. I still want to do it. I still want to have the séance, Silas. I trust you."

"It is not me you need to trust. You must trust in yourself. Your eagerness to speak to your mother could make you reckless. Patience. Discernment. Vigilance. All the things that represent your weaknesses are the very things that must become your strengths. We will begin the ceremony at 12:13 a.m. I cannot say how long it will continue or if we will find success. I can only provide an environment conducive to communication. Coraline Moon will have to do her part."

At the mention of my mother's name, the moon symbol in the center of the star seems to glow. I point wordlessly.

The milky haze evaporates from my mentor's eyes, and he straightens to his full height. "Your mother is indeed eager to speak to you."

"You saw it too? I didn't imagine it, right?"

"Trust in all your abilities. Do not leave room

for doubt or insecurity. You recognized the signs that your mother had a message for you, and now you've uncovered a way to reach through the veil. That is not a coincidence, Mizithra. That is evidence of your growth."

His shoulders return to their normal stoop, and he harrumphs. "Now, I suggest you rest and restore your strength before this evening's ceremony. It will take as long as it takes, and once we begin, we must maintain strict protocols until the spirit finishes communicating. There is no room for error. No room for dozing off. I shall see you again at midnight."

With that, he scoops up a stack of books from the table behind him and trudges down the stairs.

I'd love to take him up on his nap idea, but the excitement bubbling in my stomach probably isn't in the mood for a snooze.

Better give Erick a quick call and make sure he still wants in on this crazy idea of mine. As usual, I don't think he really has any idea what he's agreed to.

He may completely freak out once he hears how totally *Supernatural* this night is going to be.

CHAPTER 14

As THE BOOKCASE door slides open, I'm treated to an unbelievable scene.

The glamorous Ghost-ma darts around the room like a spooky cartoon character in *Scooby Doo*, while my fiendish feline bounds up and over furniture with the skill of a superhero.

In fact, he appears to be wearing a cape!

Wait, he's holding something in his toothy jaws, and it's trailing behind him. The frantic pair pays me no mind.

"Excuse me. Excuse me! What in all of Disney's haunted mansion is going on here?"

Grams freeze frames and turns toward me. Furious flames flicker in her eyes. "That infuriating animal has absconded with a valuable Hermès!"

As deadpan as I can manage, I reply, "Oh, so all of this nonsense is in response to a couture crisis?"

Something about my delivery breaks through her panic. Grams laughs so hard she ghost-snorts, and a bit of ectoplasm leaks from her nose.

The quick shift in the room's energy definitely confuses Pyewacket. He slinks toward me for protection.

Crouching, I extend my hand and speak to him in my very best sweet baby voice. "Come here, Mr. Cuddlekins. Let me see what you have. Is it a clue? Do you need me to log it into evidence?"

With each phrase, he ventures nearer. My plan works, and he releases the scarf into my waiting hands.

Ghost-ma pantomimes fainting onto an invisible Victorian couch and sighs with otherworldly relief.

"All right, I've rescued said scarf. Now, will someone please tell me what is so important about this rag?" I spin the piece of fabric like a propeller as I speak.

Pyewacket is the first to respond. "Reeeee-ow." A warning.

"Well, the fur baby clearly feels it's important to my investigation. What's your side of the story, Isadora?"

"That scarf cost more than your first car!"

"False. Prior to my inheritance, I never owned a car. What else have you got?"

She sticks out a curvy hip and firmly plants a fist. Well, as firmly as one can plant a ghost fist on an ethereal hip. "Look here, young lady. I may have exited your plane of existence with a small fortune to my name, but I didn't amass it by accident. I took care of my luxurious couture, and pairing signature pieces with exquisite accessories is how I kept everyone guessing."

Grabbing two corners of the scarf, I shake it out and suck a sharp breath between my teeth when I see the holes left by Mr. Cuddlekins' teeth. "Sorry, Grams. It looks like Pyewacket got the best of this one."

She zips across the room in a blur of energy. "Oh, dear! That was a limited edition Hermès! Irreplaceable!"

In my mind, I *couldn't* care less. I'm sure you've heard people say, "I could care less," but that implies that you could actually care *less*. In matters of damaged scarves, I actually couldn't care less.

"I heard that, Missy."

Tilting my head and narrowing my gaze, I point a single finger to my closed mouth. "Actually, the only way you could've heard that is if you were thought-dropping! Which, as you know, is strictly forbidden. So, did you hear something?"

Grams crosses her arms over her ample bosom, bites her lower lip, and shakes her head. "I must've been mistaken."

"Exactly." Wadding the scarf into a ball, I walk toward the closet.

Grams zooms in front of me and attempts to take enough corporeal form to halt my progress. "Mizithra! That is no way to care for a Hermès!" After which, she snatches the scarf from my hands and folds it with an elaborate, mind-boggling rolling and accordion nonsense. She returns it to its box in a specially built-in drawer in the closet.

"Now that the precious life of your crusty old scarf has been saved—"

"Crusty! That scarf is one hundred percent *epaisse* silk. They harvest each thread from a separate silkworm, and each scarf takes more than a year to craft. The quality is unmatched."

I roll my eyes. "Anywho, I came up here to update the murder wall." Using my sweet baby voice in a clearly patronizing tone, I continue, "Would you like to hear what we've discovered?"

After a moment of otherworldly grumbling, she replies, "Certainly."

All fashion-based crimes are forgotten, and

Grams eagerly claps her hands together while Pyewacket sits as proudly as any show cat.

Before I have a chance to give directions, she's holding the pen and hovering above the stack of 3 x 5 cards. "Who's on your list?"

"No new suspects. Just new information." I bring her up to date on Janet's attempt to flee and our discovery of her diagnosis.

Grams quickly scribbles the updates on a card and floats it toward me. "It sounds as though this Janet is exceptionally intelligent. I'm sure she made a wonderful assistant. She's detail-oriented and uniquely able to focus on the task at hand. I'm sure she'll have no trouble finding another job. You might even think about bringing her onboard at the bookshop, sweetie."

"What? Why? You know Twiggy doesn't play nice with others."

"Oh, I know, dear. But Twiggy won't be here forever. And when she retires, you'll need someone to run things." She attempts a fond smile. "You're not exactly—"

"Careful. Think very carefully about what you're going to say next." I tilt my head and stare daggers at the ghost of my benefactor.

She blinks innocently and averts her gaze. "Well, we both know you can do anything you put your mind to. You're so great at solving these crimes for Erick—"

At the mention of Erick, a certain uncomfortable conversation pops to mind. "He said I'd have to quit."

Grams closes her eyes and shakes her head as though trying to dislodge something from her ears. "He said what?"

"Erick said if we got married—"

A ghostly squeal breaks the sound barrier. "Oh, my goodness! You completely buried the lead, Mitzy! He proposed? Is the ring enormous?" She flits toward me like a hummingbird on crack and attempts to grab my left hand.

Yanking my hand free and hiding it behind my back, I try to get back on track. "First of all, the word was *if*, and no, he did not propose. Second of all, if he had, the ring would be on my right hand! As I've explained to you many times, the moody mood ring wants to be where the moody mood ring wants to be. And it's apparently rather obsessed with the ring finger of my left hand."

Her energy fades, and she nearly flickers from existence. After she floats back a pace or two, I resume my story.

"As I was saying, he indicated that IF—" I pause and arch my eyebrows for emphasis "—if we got married, I would have to cease with my amateur sleuthing. He said it was one thing for the sheriff's girlfriend to poke her nose where it didn't belong, but if I was his wife, it would absolutely be unacceptable."

Grams throws her shimmering limbs in the air and howls her disdain. "Men! They always think they have everything figured out. It's not like he would need a job if he married you. You're loaded! Why doesn't he quit his job and come to work at the bookshop?"

As soon as the sentence is out of her mouth, we both crack up.

"Grams, be serious. Erick Harper is the sheriff of Birch County. It's not a coincidence or a happy accident. It's his destiny. He couldn't possibly have a more perfect job. Plus, there's no way I'm going to allow him to pull out of the election and leave Paulsen running unopposed!"

Grams taps a finger on her flawless lips. "Good point, sweetie. But we like her a little bit now, right?"

"I guess. I mean, we made some headway when we went on that canoe rescue. But that's a different kettle of fish, Grams. Don't change the subject. Erick has to win the election. End of story."

She nods supportively. "I absolutely agree, dear.

Now, back to the update. What else did you learn about this Janet woman?"

"That was it. Oh, but I did convince Erick to sneak out to the Barnes estate with me tonight and dig up whatever Clyde was burying."

"Wait? Burying? Was there a second murder?"

I smack the palm of my hand against my forehead. "Sorry, Grams, I got distracted with the ghost antics." I nod, and she grins. "When I went there to have another look at the place where they found the body, and maybe get some information about where things actually took place, I interrupted Clyde burying something in the garden/Halloween cemetery."

She gasps and covers her mouth with a ring-ensconced hand. "Who was it?"

"Simmer down. It wasn't a body. There wasn't another murder. It was something small. I was going to go out there and dig it up myself, but I talked Erick into coming with me!"

"Well done, sweetie."

"Oh, and I had a whole vision thing. I should've told Silas before he left, but the whole séance thing threw me for a loop. You stay right there. I'm gonna call Silas and put him on speakerphone. That way, I'll only have to tell the story once."

She looks as though she's lounging on the antique four-poster bed, but there's always something that makes me uneasy when I see her floating above furniture.

Pushing that out of my mind, I call my mentor and give him the play-by-play of my strange "through the killer's eyes" vision out at the Barnes estate.

CHAPTER 15

WHILE GRAMS AND I are distracted with our phone call, the ever-entitled Pye returns to the closet and yanks the scarf out of the drawer. My only sign of trouble is a screech from Ghost-ma followed by a dangerous snarl from Pye.

The shocking sound alarms the usually calm, cool, and collected Silas Willoughby. "Mizithra, is everyone safe and accounted for?"

"Everything's fine, Silas. Grams and Pyewacket are having a whole thing over this stupid Herman scarf."

"Do you perhaps mean Hermès?"

"Sure. However you say it, it's a bunch of fancy silk—" As soon as the word *silk* passes through my lips for the umpteenth time, I remember a little tidbit from the medical examiner's report. "Wait!

As usual, Pyewacket is a step ahead! The fiber they found on the body was one hundred percent silk. Erick said it was burnt sienna, with flecks of black and gold."

The ghostly eyes of my grandmother seem to swell and glow with an energy all their own. "Are you sure it was burnt sienna? Could it possibly have been carnelian?"

Shrugging, I reply, "I haven't seen the report, Grams. Erick said burnt sienna or something. And regardless, I doubt the medical examiner worked for the Pantone color standard company. Does it matter?"

She lifts her chin and scoffs heartily. "Does it matter? My dear, would Hermès employ hundreds of color specialists to painstakingly select the pallets for their sought-after scarves if it didn't matter? If the color was carnelian with flecks of black and gold, then it is quite likely from the 1992 silk scarf release of the instant classic, *Memoires d'Hermès.*"

My shoulders shrug of their own free will. "And why would I care?"

"Don't take that tone with me." Grams adjusts a strand of pearls and inhales dramatically. "You should care, because a scarf like that would be hundreds of dollars outside the price range of a Janet Ferro."

"So, what are you saying? That the fiber automatically rules out Janet as a suspect?"

Silas harrumphs and interrupts my tiff with grams. "What is it, Silas?"

"I must admit, I'm only getting half of the story, but would you be so kind as to ask your grandmother if this particular scarf could've been something in the collection of Lillian Barnes?"

Grams gasps. "Not only could it have been—it was! I distinctly remember her wearing the scarf! Mitzy, someone from the estate would have access to Lillian's possessions. It's been more than a year since she passed. All of her things would've been processed by the trustee, given to charity, or pillaged by the help!"

"Easy, Georgia Frontiere." I lift a finger to silence Ghost-ma while I update Silas.

"All right, Grams. If you're sure this could've come from a scarf Lillian Barnes may have owned, then that puts Clyde and Mrs. Charles back on the suspect list in a big way. I don't think I can wait for Erick. Clyde knows I saw him burying an item. If he was attempting to hide the murder weapon—"

A booming voice echoes from my cell phone, "Mizithra Achelois Moon! I forbid you from venturing out to the Barnes estate unaccompanied!"

I hate to break it to Silas, but forbidding me

from doing something is about the quickest way to make it happen.

Grams attempts to intervene with what she's pulled from inside my mind, but I hold up a finger in warning. "I'm not going to be unaccompanied. Pye, would you like to go for a ride with mama?"

If caracals can snicker, he does. However, he nods his proud chin, and I most assuredly have a companion.

"It's official, Silas. Pyewacket will tag along as my bodyguard. I think it's far safer to head out there before sunset. There's precious little daylight left in almost-Canada, but I'll take what I can get."

Pressing *end* before Silas can protest, is certainly improper manners. I'll be chided for it later. No time to worry about that now.

"Pyewacket, let's hit the road." Grabbing the keys to my Jeep, a warm jacket, and my new favorite striped knit scarf, I hurry down the circular staircase and risk hopping over the chain.

It's a bit of a good news/bad news situation. Good news: I land on my feet. Bad news: the tail of the scarf catches on the chain and yanks my head back so hard I hit the right side of my noggin on the banister. Luckily, my head appears to be made of concrete, and I shake it off.

My crafty caracal and I proceed to the vehicle and make haste to the Barnes estate.

Parking out front is absolutely not an option. Clyde watches over the entrance with the eyes of a hawk. I've already tipped my hand by parking in the employee lot once before, so it might be best if I ditch the vehicle on the side of the road and see if Pyewacket can lead me to that hidden garden gate on the rear of the property.

Turning into the verge about a quarter mile before the estate, I drop a couple of tires off the shoulder.

After carefully explaining my plan to a cat—I know, I can't believe it either—we exit the vehicle, and Robin Pyewacket Goodfellow leads me into the deep, dark woods.

The sun is fading fast in the late-fall sky, and I can barely keep up. If not for the aid of my psychic senses, I would have lost the silent feline's trail immediately. Fortunately, I'm not too stressed to employ my extrasensory gifts, and, in no time at all, we arrive safely at the rear gate.

Slipping in, Pyewacket leads me off the main path through the dense hedges along the far wall. Leaves stick in my hair, branches tug at my stupid scarf, and I'm beginning to wonder if this super-stealthy route is more of a punishment than a necessity.

Eventually, the Halloween décor pops into view.

Pye slinks to the side and appears to take up the watchdog position. Oh dear! Do not tell him I said that! For the record, it's absolutely a watch-CAT position.

Ducking low, I shuffle through the foam gravestones toward the spot where I interrupted Clyde and his shovel.

Blerg. In all my careful preparation, I didn't bring a shovel!

Good thing I'm not one to spend money on manicures, because these fingernails are about to get grubby.

Digging in the freshly loosened earth, it takes less time than I imagined to reach the buried object.

The second my fingers encounter the item, I know what it is!

Pye growls in what I assume is agreement.

Carefully pulling it from the earth, I exhale with dismay when my eyes verify what my psychic senses already know.

One hundred percent silk. 1992 limited edition scarf. Hermès.

A wildcat's hiss snaps me out of my psychic reverie.

Before I can process Pyewacket's urgent warning, a thick arm encircles my neck like a boa constrictor, and blackness swallows me.

CHAPTER 16

As CONSCIOUSNESS and air seep back into my body, I remain motionless. If you know me, you know this isn't my first hostage-related rodeo. I'm not about to gasp for air and bolt upright like a soap-opera actress.

Before I tip my hand and open my eyes, I'll use my other four regular senses and all of my extra abilities to gather as much intel as possible.

There's an earthy aroma, but not damp earth, so I think we can rule out the buried alive trope!

As relief trickles through my extremities, I note the bindings securing my wrists and ankles.

Yeesh. That's unfortunate.

There are no mechanical sounds. No motors. No fans. No automobiles.

A brisk wind rustles the trees, and—

Pyewacket! He tried to warn me. I sure hope he got away.

Time to open my eyes and talk to Clyde.

Yes, Clyde is the one who put the sleeper hold on me in the garden. Despite my efforts to find another suspect, the evidence is certainly mounting against him. His fingerprint on the button in the Halloween coffin, burying the murder weapon . . . I would never have pegged him for murder.

Gently cracking the crusty seal on my eyelids, I peer into the darkness. A compact, battery-operated lantern sits on what appears to be a potting bench.

Copy that. I'm being held prisoner in the garden shed. Not exactly Alcatraz. If I can slip out of these bindings—

"I'm sorry, Miss Moon."

At least I haven't been gagged. "Clyde, what's going on? Why did you attack me?"

He wrings his large hands together.

Strange, I never took note of his solid frame and thick arms until they sealed off my airway. "She's all I have. Nobody wants someone like me. She takes care of me."

It doesn't take a psychic to realize he's talking about his mother, Mrs. Charles.

"Clyde, until today, I wouldn't have agreed with you. I always thought you were a kind, thoughtful man. Any woman would be lucky to have someone like you to share their life. Why are you so sure your mother is the only one who wants you?"

He sinks onto a rickety wooden stool that creaks dangerously under his weight. "The kids used to make fun of me at school. They called me clumsy Clyde, or Clydesdale, or—crazy Clyde."

"Hey, you don't have to explain to me how cruel kids can be. I had a horrible time with my stupid white hair and my whole orphan thing. I got picked on, called names, and definitely got into more than my share of fights. I didn't start any of them, but I was happy to finish 'em." It's hard to keep a hint of pride from my voice. I may have been small for my age back in those days, but I was scrappy and determined.

Clyde rubs his hands over his face and chokes back a dry sob. "Did I hurt you, Miss Moon? Oh, I couldn't bear it if I hurt you."

"No harm done. I'm all right, Clyde. Can we take the ropes off my wrists and ankles?"

His moment of tender regret vanishes. "I can't do that, Miss Moon."

"You can call me Mitzy." Any way to break through his shell and form some sort of camaraderie will benefit me in the negotiation.

"No, ma'am. That would be improper. My— Mrs. Charles taught me to be proper above all else."

Great. I'm stuck in the garden shed with a

mildly delusional murderer. Grams will be furious, and Erick will certainly use this incident as ammunition to prove his earlier point. "Clyde, did you kill Cheryl?"

He reflexively shakes his head in denial, but his mouth breaks rank. "Yes. I did it."

"Why? You barely even knew her. What possible reason would you have to kill her?"

The question actually confounds him. Clearly, he thought confessing to the crime would be the end. Every fiber of my psychic being screams Clyde is innocent. But if he's protecting his mother, I don't think that's a wall that even Gorbachev could bring down.

Silence hangs in the stale air, and Clyde continues to wring his hands. I sense his anxiety increasing.

"Clyde, is Pyewacket, my cat, all right? You didn't hurt the cat, did you?"

He turns and extends his left forearm. There are three deep, bloodied scratches. "I swung at him, but he got away."

Inside my head, I do a secret happy dance and give a *Woot! Woot!* for my wildcat. If I know that beast, and I'm getting to know him better every day, he's more than halfway back to Pin Cherry, and he'll bring help soon.

Thunder cracks above us, and a deluge dumps

from the heavens. Its assault on the roof is more furious than simple rain.

My captor tilts his head and hugs his arms around himself. "Hail. Hail before the full moon means death is coming soon."

Of all the creepy, obscure proverbs he could utter! I've never heard this one, but I certainly don't want to stick around and see if it comes true.

A shiver rushes over me as the intensity of the hail doubles. My poor fur baby! I hope he made it back before the storm let loose. Even a brave caracal like Pyewacket isn't going to make any progress during an unseasonal hailstorm.

Looks like it's going to be up to me and my possibly silver—or at least tin-plated—tongue.

"Clyde, can I be completely honest with you? Will you promise not to get upset?"

He dabs a dirty rag at the claw marks on his left arm. "I'll try, Miss Moon."

"Actually, put a pin in that. We should clean that wound. I don't want you to get an infection, or worse. Doc Ledo always makes sure Pyewacket is up-to-date on his shots, but cat claws aren't exactly clean. Do you have any fresh water and maybe some alcohol?"

Clyde stands and surveys the garden shed. "There's some hydrogen peroxide that we keep on the bench for the roots. That would work, wouldn't it, Miss Moon?"

"Yes. That would work great. But you need to use a clean rag. Do you have one of those?"

He scans the bench and the nearest set of shelves, but comes up empty. "Everything's been used in the garden."

"Take my scarf. It's pretty clean." I dip my chin toward the striped scarf, but shock sets in when I discover it's no longer around my neck. "I was wearing a scarf. Did you take it off?"

He shakes his head and won't meet my eyes. "The cat took it."

Score another one for Mr. Cuddlekins! Not only did he escape, but he took some proof of life. My furry overlord is going to be insufferable if I make it out of this alive. "All right. Just pour the hydrogen peroxide into the cuts, and maybe you can use a bit of your shirt tail."

While he does his best to clean the wound with our limited supplies, I take stock of any weapons of opportunity. I'm disinclined to hurt Clyde, but if we get down to a "him or me" situation, I'm going to put all my chips on me.

"Is it all right if I keep talking while you work on that?"

"Yes, Miss Moon."

"Please remember I asked you not to get upset, Clyde."

He nods and continues to fuss with his arm.

"If you're protecting Mrs. Charles, you don't have to. If she had an altercation with Cheryl, you need to let her explain herself to the sheriff. You can't take responsibility for something you didn't do, Clyde. No good will come of it."

The gentle giant places the bottle of hydrogen peroxide on the workbench, screws the cap on securely, and slowly turns. "Miss Moon, I have to protect her." He gestures toward the dark corner in the back of the shed. "There's a jug of gasoline over there for the mower. I can put you to sleep like I did before and then—"

"Wait! Do not kill me, Clyde! I know you're innocent. If you burn down this garden shed, that's all gone. How do you think your mother will feel if you go to prison for actually murdering someone?"

He shrugs his shoulders and takes a step toward the gasoline can.

Time is running out, and the freak storm shows no sign of ending.

The last thing I want is to go out in a blaze of glory. No thanks!

CHAPTER 17

A STARTLING FLASH of lightning temporarily illuminates everything inside the shed, and a thick-han-
dled shovel gleams near the door. It seems like
we've reached the "him or me" portion of this
dreadful scenario.

From the great beyond, my mother's voice
comes to me. *Patience, my magical princess. You'll
get this sorted, Mippity Bippity Boo.*

Mama? Magical princess? My heart aches in
my chest, and, suddenly, I want nothing more than
to survive long enough to have that séance. Maybe
she means the alchemy stuff. I have no idea if the
alchemical exercise Silas taught me to get myself
out of metal handcuffs will work on rope, but I'm
absolutely going to try.

First, I need to buy myself some time. "Hold on.

Hold on. Let's take a minute to think things through, Clyde. You finish cleaning up that arm of yours, and I'll see if I can think of a way to make everything all right." There's no world in which things are going to be all right, and I feel a flash of guilt for taking advantage of his trusting nature.

"Yes, Miss Moon."

For the record, this promises to be the most polite murder in history!

Closing my eyes, I sink into the calm space within. An exercise I would've eagerly laughed at during my days in Sedona, Arizona, could now be the ticket to saving my life.

A sense of calm washes over me, and I run through the steps in my mind. I visualize ice melting, but add another layer. There's seaweed trapped in the ice, and as the ice melts, the seaweed unwinds and finds its own freedom.

I'm barely able to contain the gasp in my throat when the rope falls from my wrists.

Step one complete. Now I have to distract him.

There aren't any logical options.

Before I can twist my brain into a pretzel, a loud voice cuts through nature's commotion.

"Clyde! Clyde Woodruff Charles! You will catch your death from this storm. I need you to bank up the fire in the kitchen this instant."

Clyde's entire demeanor changes at the bark of

his mother's voice. "I have to go. I'll be back in the morning to take care of you."

I have no idea which meaning of "take care of you" he's leaning into, but I have no intention of being here in the morning. He searches for something to cover his injured arm, but the door to the shed bursts open before he succeeds.

"Land o' Goshen! What on earth is going on, Clyde?" The normally bristly Mrs. Charles rushes to my side and yanks me to my bound feet.

I teeter precariously, and I'm forced to reveal my free hands to catch myself on the wall.

Clyde lunges forward, but his mother stops and turns him to stone with a single glance. Only his eyes blink as she removes the rope from my ankles. "I do not know what you two have gotten up to, but I do not allow Clyde to have female visitors after dark."

Fury rushes to the surface, and my adrenal glands land firmly in the *FIGHT* camp. "Are you kidding me? Do you actually think I would willingly drag myself into this disgusting shed and tie my own hands and feet?" I rub my raw wrists. "Clyde attacked me in the garden when I was digging up the murder weapon! He claims he killed Cheryl, but I think he's protecting you. If you killed Chiffon Cheryl, then you need to come clean with Sheriff Harper."

The absolute stupidity of my outburst hits me several seconds too late. I'm trapped in a garden shed with the murderer and a son willing to burn it all down to protect her. Fair play to Mrs. Charles.

Contrary to every scene I've ever watched in a horror movie, no axe emerges from behind her back. Mrs. Charles tears up and places a comforting arm around my shoulders. "Is that what he said? My dear son is willing to go to prison for me?"

"What's going on, Mrs. Charles?"

She motions for Clyde to open the door. "I think we better head into the house and discuss this terrible situation over hot cocoa and snickerdoodles."

Well, stick a fork in me. I'm done! Of all the ways I thought this situation would play out, I never imagined it would end with snickerdoodles.

Inside the staff kitchen, Mrs. Charles tends to Clyde's wound, first and foremost, and then tells her tale as she stirs up a pot of old-fashioned, home-made cocoa.

"The woman, Cheryl, came back with her assistant. There was another unpleasant scuffle, but eventually, we sorted things out, and I agreed Clyde would give her a private tour. The other one, the little one with the beady eyes, had researched the estate and wanted to see the remaining artwork. I told her the most valuable pieces had been donated to museums." She pauses to taste her brew.

"Donated to museums" is certainly an interesting interpretation of events, but there's no time to debate semantics.

"I escorted her to the gallery of the masters and told her to come back downstairs once she'd finished." Mrs. Charles loads a plate with snickerdoodles. "I had cookies in the oven and pie crust dough in the fridge. I lost track of time and eventually realized she hadn't come downstairs. So, I walked out to the garden to find Clyde and Cheryl, and see if perhaps the little one had joined them."

Clyde swallows audibly and shuffles his feet.

"When I opened the door, I saw Clyde standing over Cheryl's body, with the scarf in his hands."

Mind blown. Every fiber of my psychic being felt sure of Clyde's innocence. "Are you saying Clyde killed Cheryl?"

Her ladle clatters to the floor, and she shakes her head violently as she presses a hand to her chest. "No, certainly not! He wouldn't. He couldn't." Tears once again leak from her eyes.

On the one hand, she's proclaiming his innocence, but clearly, she has doubts.

Mrs. Charles swipes at her tears and continues. "We didn't have time to talk about things. I assumed the worst and asked him to help me hide the body.

He must've thought I'd had something to do with it—"

"Clyde, is that true? Did you think your mother had something to do with Cheryl's death?"

He rubs at the fresh bandage on his left arm and remains silent.

"Do either of you know if the scarf was one of Lillian's?"

Mrs. Charles had stooped to recover the ladle, but she shot to her full height with surprising speed. "Who told you that?"

Think. Think. Think. It's not like I can out Ghost-ma. "It looked expensive. I assumed."

She wipes the stain from the floor and decants the hot chocolate. Without responding, she places the mugs on the stout table beside me and sets a plate of cookies in the middle. It would be comical if it weren't so frightening.

"We need to call the sheriff. I'm starting to think neither of you killed Cheryl."

Mrs. Charles and her son both stare at me for a moment. Then their eyes meet. She hurries toward him as he weeps. Her tears join his, and I feel relief flood through the room.

"So, if Clyde thought he was covering for you, and you thought you were covering for Clyde . . . Who killed Cheryl?"

The front door of the mansion bursts open to

the tune of splintering wood, and we all turn in shock.

Shouting past my mouthful of cookie, I greet the new arrival. "Erick!"

His gun is drawn, and his face twists with worry.

Paulsen skirts around him, gun also drawn, and comes straight for the three of us.

It's good to know certain things will never change.

Eager to lighten the mood, I pick up the plate of cookies and shove them toward her. "Snickerdoodle, Deputy?"

CHAPTER 18

PAULSEN LUNGES in my general direction and holds the plate of treats at gunpoint.

The sheriff is a little quicker on the uptake. Erick assesses the situation and holsters his weapon. He lifts both hands in the air and offers me the universal sign for confused frustration. "Can someone tell me what's going on? A wild animal broke into my station dragging your stupid Harry Potter scarf and growled at me until I loaded him into my cruiser!" He presses a hand to his forehead and takes a deep breath. "I thought you were—"

Dropping the plate of cookies on the table, I rush to his side. "I could've been. I almost was!"

His teeth grind as he stares daggers at Mrs. Charles and her progeny. "I'm going to need the whole story. Better yet, Paulsen, take Dottie and Clyde down to the station."

Dottie? Color me shocked. It never occurred to me that Mrs. Charles has a first name.

Mrs. Charles turns to the stove and puts a cover over the remaining hot chocolate. She then removes her apron, washes her hands, and crosses her arms over her chest. "Clyde and I will accompany Deputy Paulsen willingly." She hooks an arm through her son's elbow. "We have nothing to hide."

Erick must sense the relief in her voice. He tilts his head toward me, and I roll my eyes like wild pinballs and shake my head in response.

"Take them in, Paulsen. No booking, just get their statements—officially." He tilts his head toward the mother and son. "There are definitely some pieces missing, but I think the two of you know more than you told me the first time I came out here."

Clyde nods his head toward Erick in a way that insinuates he's doffing a cap.

Note to self: Did Erick jack that move from Clyde, or vice versa?

The large man presses his lips together firmly before commenting. "Sorry about that, Sheriff Harper. We'll tell Deputy Paulsen everything—this time."

Erick rolls his shoulders back and exhales. "Moon, you're with me. That crazy animal is in my backseat. I'm telling you right now, if he does anything to that upholstery—"

"Don't worry, Sheriff. Mr. Cuddlekins is a furry angel. And if for some reason I'm wrong about that, the Duncan-Moon Foundation will see that the department receives a new cruiser."

The hint of a grin lifts one corner of his mouth, but he refuses to give up that easily. He's still salty, and he wants me to know it. "For now, you'll be sitting in back with your beast."

"Happy to." There's definitely no way I'm going to let him believe he's got the upper hand.

Paulsen loads up her interview subjects and heads out. As soon as her taillights disappear, Erick scoops me into his arms and squeezes me so tight . . .

"Air. I—can't—breathe."

He chuckles and loosens his hold a fraction of an inch. "This has got to stop, Mitzy. When Pyewacket weaseled his way into the station . . . that dirty scarf hanging from his . . . My heart stopped beating for a full minute! I can't lose you. You get that, right?"

"You're never gonna lose me, Erick. I'm like a bad penny. I always come back."

He leans down and kisses me.

See, he can't stay angry with me. There's tender

love on his lips, but the singular emotion that floods my senses when our energy collides is fear.

"I thought I lost you. You've gotten yourself into trouble before, but—something about that scarf—just hanging there . . ."

Pushing to my tiptoes, I kiss him passionately and pull away. "What time is it?"

He scoffs, wipes a tear from his eye, and shakes his head. "Seriously? I'm giving you my best stuff here, Moon."

I tighten my arms around him and squeeze until he groans. "I'll take your best stuff any day of the week, Harper. But we're supposed to be at a séance at midnight."

"Okay. Load up." He walks me out of the accursed manor and opens the passenger-side door at the rear of the cruiser.

Pyewacket lunges toward me. The force of his greeting knocks me backward, but Erick catches me.

Climbing into the back with Pye, I snuggle him, scratch between his tufted ears, and praise him endlessly.

The adoration pleases him. There's a rumbling that resembles a purr, and the tuft of his left ear tickles my cheek as he nuzzles me affectionately.

"You should've seen the deputies when that thing walked into the bullpen." Erick chuckles.

"Yeah, Pyewacket knows how to control a room."

"Reow." Can confirm.

"Johnson ran straight to the bathroom and locked himself in. Gilbert jumped up on top of his desk and drew his gun." Erick laughs as he recalls the commotion. "Paulsen was the only one who held it together."

"Pyewacket, did you cause trouble at the sheriff's station?"

"RE-OW!" Game on!

"He would never hurt anyone. He was only trying to get your attention, Ricky."

Erick's eyes dart to the rearview mirror, and the light from the dashboard illuminates the fear that lingers there. "Don't ever scare me like that again. Promise?"

Now doesn't seem like the time to have this discussion. Grams made some valid points about me having the right to do what makes me happy, but relationships are ultimately about workable compromises. Maybe my mother will have some additional words of wisdom from the great beyond.

"Moon? Did I lose you?"

"For the millionth time, you're not going to lose me. I mean, I do occasionally get distracted by my mind movies, but I'm not going anywhere. Plus, I took precautions. Pyewacket accompanied me to the estate as a bodyguard, and he did exactly what he was supposed to do. When Clyde grabbed me, Pyewacket gave him a THWACK he won't soon forget and went for help."

Erick slams on the brakes, and I barely get my hand up in time to prevent hitting the wire mesh divider. "What are you talking about? You were sitting in the kitchen having hot chocolate and cookies. Clyde grabbed you?"

Against my better judgment, I relay the events in the garden and the additional events in the garden shed.

I'm choosing to censor Erick's colorful commentary and cut straight to his more lucid questions once he resumes driving toward Pin Cherry.

"So you found the murder weapon?"

"For a hot minute. When I woke up in the garden shed, it was gone."

Erick depresses the button on his mic. "Sheriff Harper for dispatch."

"Go for dispatch."

"Get a note to Deputy Paulsen. She's taking a statement from Dottie and Clyde. She needs to make sure they reveal the location of the murder weapon. An expensive silk scarf. Over."

"10-4."

Erick eases his vehicle down the alley and turns off the engine. "I called Clarence about your Jeep.

He'll tow it to his yard. I can take you over there to-morrow if he doesn't have time to drop it off."

"Thanks." I smile and nod, but something else is bothering me. "Hey, you're not actually gonna charge the Charleses?" The phrase makes me snicker, and the theme song from *Charles in Charge* instantly plays in my head. I can't contain my giggles.

"We could charge Clyde with unlawful imprisonment for holding you in that shed. Or charge both of them with interfering in an investigation and tampering with evidence, but if they tell us everything, we probably won't. But why is charging them funny?" Erick puts his arm across the front seat and turns to peer at me through the mesh.

Singing the theme song as terribly as I'm able: "I want Charles in charge of me—" I choke on the lyrics. "Ewww. That's kind of a pervy song. I never real—"

Without commenting, he exits the vehicle, walks around the back of the car, and pauses outside my door before leaning down. His handsome face glows in the moonlight.

I smile and paw at the window like a One Direction groupie.

"Moon, give me one good reason why you couldn't wait for me to accompany you to the Barnes estate as we agreed?"

Scowling, I reach for the door handle and find none. Touché, Sheriff Harper. He clearly plans to leave me trapped in the criminal compartment until I meet his demands. Fine.

"I was worried Clyde might try to move the thing. I interrupted him while he was burying it. I didn't want to take a chance on losing what might've been—and turned out to be—the murder weapon."

Erick leans closer to the glass. "But you're more than happy to take a chance on losing your life?"

Advantage: Harper. I'm not about to let him know it.

"We can discuss the particulars later. Pyewacket is hungry, and I have to get upstairs. Tonight might be my only chance to talk to my mother. Please? Please, let me out?"

At the mention of my mother, Erick immediately opens the door and offers me his hand.

Pyewacket darts out and scratches at the metal door leading into the bookshop from the alleyway. The door opens of its own accord, and I hear Grams cooing with delight at the arrival of her precious caracal.

Maybe tonight I'll have the chance to rejoice over the arrival of my sweet, innocent mother.

When we walk into the bookshop, Grams doesn't zoom toward me. My first instinct is to feel insulted, but then I realize she's not upset because she doesn't know what happened. My second instinct is to keep the details from her until after the séance. Lucky for me, she's so busy doling out ghost kisses to Pyewacket that she takes no notice of Erick and me as we move past them and climb the circular staircase to the Rare Books Loft.

When Erick catches sight of the massive pentacle carved on the floor, he takes a step back and grips the thick balustrade. "What have you gotten me into?"

Silas emerges from the shadows, and a soothing voice seems to push a breeze of calm across the mezzanine. "There is nothing to fear, Sheriff. The workings of the séance have existed for generations. I have taken every precaution to protect Mitzy."

Erick turns to me and rubs a hand across his forehead. "So, she really could be in danger?"

"Don't overreact, Erick. There's nothing to worry about. Silas is extremely careful. There's just that tiniest, most minuscule possibility that when I open myself up to communicate with my mother, some other entities might try to put their two cents in. It's not a big deal. We totally have it under control."

Erick shakes his head and clicks his tongue. "Silas, can you guarantee that Mitzy will be safe?"

My mentor steps forward and places a hand on

Erick's shoulder. "My dear Mr. Harper, there are no guarantees in life. There are even fewer in death. Mitzy's abilities are rare, and it would be irresponsible of me to assume I know the entirety of their complexities." Erick opens his mouth, but Silas squeezes his shoulder and continues. "However, I have been exploring these forces since before you were born. I would lay down my life before I would allow harm to come to Mizithra."

Erick nods, and I, of course, cry.

Silas offers me his handkerchief and touches a finger under my chin. "Take a moment to gather your thoughts. If you need some water, or tea, or just a minute to yourself, you must do so now. Once we begin the séance, no one can leave the pentacle. We shall all place our hands on the symbol of the moon at its center. It is imperative that our hands remain locked in place until I end the ritual. Do you both understand?"

My boyfriend shrugs and nods halfheartedly.

"Copy that, Silas. I'm going to take a minute. How long till we start?"

He pulls a pocket watch from his fusty tweed coat, flips open the cover, and harrumphs. "Ten minutes, exactly."

I elbow Erick in the side. "Good thing you got to the mansion when you did. Cutting it pretty close, pal."

He puts both his hands in the air as though it's an old-fashioned stickup and shakes his head. "I'm all out of comebacks, Moon. Take whatever time you need. I'll be waiting for you."

Reaching toward him, I squeeze his hand and wink. "Thanks, Sheriff."

CHAPTER 19

CAREFULLY SKIRTING THE PENTACLE, I reach up and pull the candle handle. Silas continues to explain the basics of otherworldly spirit communication to Erick as the door slides closed behind me.

Alone, for the first time since the hostage crisis, my bravado fades faster than a summer vacation tan.

Collapsing onto the overstuffed settee, tears sluice down my cheeks. Before the pity party can really take off, the mood ring on my left hand encircles my finger in an icy chill.

As I look down through watery eyes, a memory unfolds of my young mother applying mascara to her eyelashes, and playfully kissing my nose.

The anticipation of speaking to her tonight, maybe seeing her ghost—it erases all the trauma from my recent kidnapping encounter. Glancing at my dirty T-shirt and stained skinny jeans, I squeak with fright.

"Myrtle Isadora Johnson Linder Duncan Willamet Rogers! If you ever loved me, you'll get your ethereal rear end in here on the double and help make me presentable."

The final words of the sentence still hang in the air when Grams bursts through the wall. "I heard the cry of a fashion emergency. What do you need?"

"I need the perfect outfit for seeing my mother for the first time in thirteen years! And, Grams, there are no rules. You get in that closet, and you go hog-wild!"

She whoops like a rodeo cowgirl and zips into the closet.

I strip off my stinky outer layer and take what's known as a whore's bath. Although to be fair, it used to be a pretty typical bath when I was a broke barista living in a rundown apartment with totally intermittent hot water. So you could say I'm kind of an expert—in the *bath* part—not the other part!

After my speedy wash-up, I apply an elegant amount of makeup. I'm tempted to use my mother's favorite mocha lip tint, but I'm feeling daring. Instead, I select a tube of Passionate Plum Frost and smile when I catch my reflection.

I'm all grown up. Will she be proud of the woman I've become? Will she like my hair?

Speaking of, my snow-white strands stick up in all directions. Time to get to work with the styling wand. My locks have grown out a bit, despite my frequent amateur trimmings. So, I can almost manage slight beachy waves. Ghost-ma's help would make it better, but I don't dare distract her from the wardrobe portion of this quick change.

As if on cue, a commanding voice echoes from the intercom speaker. "Two minutes left, Mizithra."

One last look in the mirror, and I nod somewhat approvingly.

"Mitzy, get in here!" Grams' frantic voice pierces through the wall.

I race into the closet and stop cold. "That's the exact same outfit you picked out when I met Jacob. I mean, Dad."

She crosses her arms and smiles warmly. "Why not? You like it. It's extremely flattering. And I figured if it works for one of your amazing parents, it has to work for the other. Plus" —she floats over the padded mahogany bench and sidles up next to me— "you're going to be sitting on the floor for quite a while. I think you'll be happy in black skinny jeans. And the striped boyfriend sweater will keep you from freezing to death in the wee hours."

I throw my arms around her ethereal shape and

manage what passes for a hug in our book. "I can't wait for you to meet her."

Isadora arches a perfectly plucked eyebrow. "Are you sure I'm allowed?"

"What do you mean? Of course you're allowed. In fact, I insist." Ignoring her continued concern, I jump into the jeans, shove my feet into the black riding boots, and wiggle into the cozy cashmere sweater.

Grams is ghost-pacing by the time my head pops through the neck opening.

"What's going on? You want to meet my mom, don't you?"

"Did you clear it with Silas?"

A disembodied voice announces, "It's time."

"One way to find out. Follow me."

I press the twisted ivy medallion, and Grams waits behind my left shoulder as the door slides open.

When Silas reaches the top of the circular staircase, the candlelight reflects off his round spectacles —the eyewear I refer to as "ghost-vision" peepers. He takes one look at Isadora and shakes his head. "It could be quite unpredictable, Isadora. The veil is precious thin. Your tether has been rebuilt, but it may not be indestructible. I shall strongly suggest you avoid the risk. Ultimately, the decision, and the consequences thereof, reside in your hands."

"I really want her to meet my mom, Silas. Can she watch from a distance?"

He harrumphs and smooths his bushy grey mustache with thumb and forefinger. "Mizithra Achelois Moon, I am managing several uncertain possibilities simultaneously. Adding your grandmother's presence to the list of things I must monitor while you attempt to commune with the spirits is a risk I cannot take. You must choose."

Turning to the woman who has become my surrogate mother in these last few years, I repeatedly blink to keep the tears at bay and preserve my makeup. "Grams, I'm lucky enough to see you every day. This may be the only chance I have to see my mother. Can you understand?"

She throws her arms around me, but the agitation of the situation causes her phantasmal limbs to pass straight through me. I don't get goosebumps, or ghost bumps as we've come to call them, and I can sense her unrest as she says, "You made the right choice, dear. I'll be in the museum. You tell your mother how much I love you. Will you do that?"

"Absolutely. Thanks, Grams."

She pops out of the visual spectrum, and I nod toward Silas. "Looks like we're ready. What do we do now?"

He motions for Erick and me to join him in the center of the pentacle. We sit cross-legged, even my wizened mentor, in a triangular circle. He shows us how to place our hands flat against the carving of the moon in our midst, and each of us makes a triangle with our thumbs and forefingers. As our six hands press down on the symbol, our pinkies touch all the way around.

Silas, leaving his ghost spectacles on, offers a final warning. "Do not remove your hands from this symbol until I tell you it is done. If there is a danger I cannot delay, then I will close the portal to the spirit world, and there'll be no argument. Understood?"

Erick immediately agrees. "10-4."

I make a face at the sheriff. "Suck up." Nodding more seriously at our master of ceremonies, I mind my manners. "I agree, Silas."

Sheriff Harper chuckles nervously. "Will I be able to see the ghosts?"

Silas works his mustache left and right. "It is up to each individual spirit who crosses over to decide how they reveal themselves. You may ask questions when Mitzy indicates it is acceptable to do so."

Erick shrugs in my general direction, and I nod my acknowledgment.

Without further explanation, Silas inhales deeply and his stooped shoulders straighten fully. The milky blue of his eyes slips away, and the deep indigo that replaces it seems like a window to another world. "Hold the image of your mother in your mind, Mizithra. Hold it firmly. Think of no one else."

Why did he have to say that? When someone tells me to think of no one else, all I can do is think of everyone else!

Erick's pinky subtly presses against mine.

Maybe a little of my psychic ability is rubbing off on ol' Sheriff Harper. "All right, Silas, I'm thinking of her."

An image of the two of us running to the ice cream truck in the Arizona heat fills every part of my mind.

We're sitting on the curb eating orange creamsicles. The cold treat melts and drips over my nine-year-old fingers. The bells on the ice-cream truck ring out as it moves down the block. The creamy orange flavor fills my mouth. Her face—

Her face is so clear now.

"I knew you'd come for me, my magical Mitzy."

The voice I hear is not in my mind.

When my eyelids flutter open, the beautiful dark eyes of my mother and her honey-brown locks fill my entire field of vision.

Makeup be damned. Tears of joy stream down my face. "Mama, is it really you?"

The smart, playful lilt of her British accent brings more memories flooding back. "Look how you've gone and grown! You're a proper woman, now! My baby is all grown up!"

"I miss you every day. I met my dad. Jacob has hair just like mine, Mama."

"Oh, Mitzy. I'm sorry I never—"

"No regrets. Everything happens for a reason. Nod and smile. Right?"

Her soft lips turn up at the corners and she nods through her ghost tears. "When did you get so wise?"

"I remember everything you taught me. Everything."

Through her shimmering form, the almost glowing eyes of Silas meet mine. The faintest smile hangs on his lips.

"Mama, I want to introduce you to some people."

She smiles, wipes her tears, and flicks her hair behind her shoulder with one hand. "I'd be chuffed to meet anyone you deem worthy."

"The man in the glasses, with the formidable mustache, is Mr. Silas Willoughby. He's the one who found me, and he's been helping me with—" My voice catches in my throat and I'm unable to continue.

Silas peers through his round spectacles and finishes the explanation. "Miss Coraline Moon, it is a pleasure to make your acquaintance. You have a remarkable daughter, and it has been my pleasure to assist her in uncovering the depths of her psychic abilities and the possibilities that lie beyond this plane. Jacob Duncan's mother learned of your daughter's existence and insisted, in her last will and testament, that I bring Mitzy to Pin Cherry Harbor. You would be quite proud of everything your daughter has achieved. And I believe you would also approve of the man with whom she's chosen to share her heart." Silas nods, and I search for my voice.

"Mama, this is Erick Harper. He's the Sheriff and my boyfriend."

My mother flashes her eyebrows as she looks him over. "He's quite handsome. And he must treat you well. My sweet girl has standards." She points toward the badge on his chest. "Not surprising you'd pick a proper lawman. You always were a stickler for rules."

Her comment makes me laugh out loud, and I nearly lift one of my hands.

"Do not move your hands, Mizithra."

The compulsion of my mentor's voice locks my hands to the floor. "I don't want to waste any time talking about unpleasantness, Mom, but I'm not gonna lie. There were some bad years. I did some stuff."

Erick can no longer hold his tongue. "I'm

sorry. I can't actually see you, Miss Moon. But I can assure you that your daughter is still getting into plenty of trouble, if that's what you're discussing."

My mother looks at me and her sparkling eyes widen. "Mizithra?" She giggles, and there's a pop and a sizzle as her energy shifts.

Next to me, Erick startles and leans back, but keeps his hands pressed to the floor.

"Begging your pardon if I frightened you, Sheriff. The name is Coraline Moon. Pleasure to make your acquaintance."

As though he meets visiting spirits on a daily basis, Erick immediately finds his calm center. "Miss Moon, I'm not sure how long you can stay, and I've been waiting a few years to ask this question. Would you have any objection to my asking for your daughter's hand in marriage?"

My heart nearly leaps out of my chest. What the—?! Well, you should know by now, we Duncan women have our limits.

Grams rockets through the wall from the printing museum, and my hands fly from the floor. One presses against my chest, and one reaches for Erick's face.

Before my mother can answer, officially, thunder seems to crackle above our heads and lightning appears to strike inside the loft. Darkness swirls up from an abyss where the moon symbol once stood.

My mother's ghost is instantly sucked toward the vortex.

"Mama! Wait!"

"Don't fret. I'll always love you, my . . ."

And she's gone.

Silas leaps to his feet with the agility of a teenage boy. "Myrtle Isadora, I command you to leave this space at once."

Grams struggles against the pull of the dark whirlpool, and Erick yanks me backward from the growing sinkhole.

Ghost-ma is losing the battle, and her left foot is mere inches from the all-consuming blackness. I can almost hear the spirits calling to her from the other side.

I reach for her, but Erick's arms are locked around me.

Silas digs into a hidden pocket in his wrinkled coat, and I pray for an alchemical miracle.

Out of nowhere, the snarling fangs of a caracal glint as another bolt of lightning strikes inside my bookshop. Pyewacket bounds toward the growing opening as fearlessly as an entire pride of lions.

Silas throws a vial toward Pye. It shimmers with blues, greens, and gold.

The marvelous wildcat catches it in his mouth, and I cheer. Maybe we won . . .

As my brave boy leaps into the swirling black hole, his eyes gleam like moonlight and he makes a sound I've never heard. But I know as soon as the mournful cry echoes through the empty bookshop that it means—goodbye.

CHAPTER 20

ALL THE SOUND is sucked out of the room. Silas races to attend to Grams, and Erick attempts to communicate with me. His lips are moving. The movements might mean something.

These earthly concerns can't touch me. I lock my eyes on the spot on the floor where my beautiful, precious Pyewacket ceased to exist.

How do I go on? He was part of our family. I've lost so much . . . My heart will never be whole again.

With the force of a rushing ocean wave, all my senses fire up at once.

Silas implores me to translate for Grams. She's missing the designer shoe from her left foot. A chunk has been torn away from the hem of her beautiful Marchesa gown—and vanished. Erick waves a hand in front of my face and calls my name.

This isn't the séance I'd envisioned.

"Grams, are you all right?" Pushing past Erick, I fall to my knees beside the frightened ghost of my grandmother. Her energy is so drained and thin that she can't gain any corporeal form. Without thinking, I reach my right hand toward her ethereal heart and close my eyes.

Silas instinctively moves away.

It feels as though there's a string connected directly to my own heart. The thread travels down my arm and out the center of my palm. Something inside the ghost of my dear grandmother is pulling on that string.

She whispers gratefully, and I squeeze my eyes closed to hold my focus. As the minutes wear on, semi-corporeal fingers brush against my arm. The feeling of this transfer of energy is almost euphoric. My consciousness drifts from the exchange. I might be floating.

Strong hands pull me away from my grandmother. There's a painful tug as the last of our connection snaps free, and I jolt back into my body. Silas removes a small amber vial from his pocket and forces the thick greenish liquid between my lips.

"This should restore some of what was taken."

As images of the séance's horrific ending flash through my head, I grip his gnarled hand and speak through my tears. "What about Pyewacket? Did you give him one of these? Will he—" As soon as the question forms on my lips, I'm not certain I want to hear the answer.

Erick kneels beside me and places a comforting arm around my shoulders.

Grams weeps openly. However, Silas has removed his spectacles, so I'm the only one to bear witness to her pain.

"Hey, I'm sorry, Mitzy. I never would've asked your mom the question if I'd known." He gestures to the fallout. "I was trying to do the right thing."

Turning into him, I grip his shirt with both of my hands and weep.

He scoops me into his arms, and as he walks toward the apartment, Silas makes a general announcement. "We must all rest. I will remain here at the portal in case Robin Pyewacket Goodfellow is able to send a message. We mustn't rule out the wily wits of our furry compatriot."

At the mention of my fiendish feline friend, a fresh round of sobs erupts.

Erick nods, opens the bookcase door, and carries me to the bed. He attempts to pull off my boots as I instinctively curl into a fetal position.

He makes a quick phone call, which I completely ignore. The pain in my chest aches so loudly that I can hear nothing else.

Climbing onto the bed, he curves around me like the big spoon. Memories of Pyewacket consume my mind.

The first time he introduced himself and scared me half to death.

The time he scratched the living daylights out of the cupboard door under the stairs trying to stow away in my suitcase when I traveled back to Arizona.

That one time, he attacked a gypsy in defense of Grams.

The time he took a bullet for my dad and me.

Stupid. Stupid wildcat. If he'd stop trying to be the hero, he'd still be here.

The silent argument continues in my mind, and Erick's arms are the only things keeping me from absolutely falling to pieces.

It's impossible not to relive the pain of my mother's death as I struggle to process another monumental loss.

I work my way through the stages of grief multiple times. Finding the most comfort in anger. Believing sleep will never come, I press tightly against Erick, hoping his substance and solidity will keep me from disappearing.

When the wicked fingers of dawn pry my eyelids open, it only takes a heartbeat for the unpleas-antness to flood back.

As I stir, Erick instantly awakes and is on his feet. "Can I get you some coffee? Do you want me to grab something from the diner?"

Sitting up on the bed, I hug my knees to my chest. "Believe it or not, I have no appetite."

That announcement tells Erick everything he needs to know.

He drops onto the bed beside me and squeezes me against his strong chest. "I've seen you and Silas get out of much stickier situations. Let's not give up hope. Okay?"

My head nods robotically, but my broken heart has already given up on everything.

Erick gets up and gently brushes his hand along the side of my face. "I'm going to head down to the back room and make a pot of coffee. I definitely need some, and I'm sure Silas didn't sleep well either."

I nod mutely and wipe fresh tears from my cheeks as he exits.

Muffled voices from the Rare Books Loft con-firm Silas is still on site and awake before the rest of us.

Grams pops into the visible spectrum in the middle of the apartment and tilts her head in sadness. "I hope it's okay, dear. I saw Erick making coffee in the back room, so—"

My feet fall to the floor, and I shamble toward her.

The state of her dress and her missing shoe finally catch my attention. "Grams, your shoe! It's gone. You almost—"

She presses a glowing finger to my lips and shakes her head. "Mr. Cuddlekins saved me, sweetie. We must properly honor his memory. I want you to order the largest headstone in history, and I want you to have them rename the pet cemetery: the *King* and Queen of Heaven Pet Cemetery. And I want First Avenue renamed Pyewacket Avenue."

Oh brother. "I know we all deal with grief in different ways, Grams. But before we hold the wake of the century and rename everything in town, let's see if Silas has any other ideas."

When the bookcase door slides open to reveal the scene in the loft, my heart pounds like a kettle-drum and I shake my head in disbelief.

Erick lounges in the center of the pentacle, and there's something tan and furry in his lap.

Running forward, I fall to my knees and reach toward the bundle. "Pyewacket!"

A tiny hiss stops me in my tracks. A miniature paw takes a swipe at my outstretched fingers.

"What's going on? What is this?"

Erick shakes his head and nods toward Silas. "Better let the expert explain."

The caracal kitten in Erick's lap nuzzles against him with unbridled adoration. A wave of jealousy washes over me as I turn to my mentor. "Did you go out and buy me a kitten last night?"

Silas harrumphs and retrieves a chair from one of the curved arms of the mezzanine. He sits, adjusts his coat, and clears his throat. "Robin Pyewacket Goodfellow has always been a great deal more than he appears. When I saw your grandmother in grave danger, I knew he'd risk all his remaining lives and do something foolish. Unlike his previous stunts in this dimension, passing through the veil holds a radically unique set of consequences. I had to react rapidly. There was little time to weigh the pros and cons of my actions. As Pyewacket leapt toward the abyss, I threw a vial of an alchemical solution I invented myself. It's known as a dimensional anchor. One day, I hope to test it myself." He pauses and smooths his mustache. "However, based on today's results, I may reconsider." Despite the grave situation, Silas chuckles.

"What are you saying? What does an anchor do?"

"I'm glad you asked. When a living creature passes through the veil, their energy upsets the balance. They are not *of* the afterlife, yet they are in it. The goal of the anchor is to serve as a reminder of the dimension from whence they came."

"Why?"

Erick and the kitten are driving me insane with their lovey-dovey playtime. I'm starting to understand why Garfield got so upset every time the infernal Nermal came for a visit!

Silas patiently continues. "I've seen Robin Pyewacket Goodfellow accomplish far too many astonishing things. He is prescient and, I believe, has a penchant for the supernatural. He certainly communicates effectively with your grandmother and understands the nuances of human speech. After multiple lifetimes, he has achieved his most perfect form. He has no need to incarnate as anything other than himself."

"Silas, you're killing me. Can you get to the peak of *Mount What's Your Point* sometime today?"

He tilts his head, nods, and smiles. "Amusing. My point is this. I provided the anchor, Pyewacket provided the miracle." He gestures toward the tiny kitten.

Curiosity burns through my veins. Reaching toward the furry little kitty, with more caution this time, I wait until it turns and sniffs my hand. There, across the left eye, are several deep scars. "But those are Pyewacket's scars. How does this kitten—?"

Silas grins mischievously and Erick smiles like the cat who swallowed the canary—appropriately.

I swallow. "This is supposed to be Pyewacket? Reincarnated?"

Grams wanders out of the apartment, hears my query, and screeches in delight. "It worked! The soul anchor actually worked!"

She zips toward the caracal kitten and frightens the daylights out of it as she touches its back with her ghost energy.

The cat utters a sound. "Reeeew." It's not one I recognize.

"If it's Pyewacket, why can't he communicate with me? Why don't I understand him?"

Silas bobs his head and his jowls waggle. "We shall take this journey of understanding together, Mizithra. I believe it is indeed Pyewacket. However, he has been somewhat reset. The best thing we can do is love him and support him while he re-familiarizes himself with this dimension. Whether he will grow at the pace of a normal caracal kitten, or perhaps at some supernatural rate, remains to be seen. We are all quite out of our depth."

Erick smiles and scratches the kitten's belly. "I love this new version of Pyewacket. He seriously likes me. Way more than the last one."

Placing a hand on my hip, I scoff openly. "Pyewacket belongs to me—"

"And me!" Grams has taken up a similar defensive pose.

We exchange a conspiratorial nod. "Correction, Grams and me. And I don't think you need to be twisting our caracal's affections."

Erick scoops the tiny beast close to his T-shirt-covered chest and walks toward me. "Okay. But he does like me best."

The tiny beast emits a whispery, "Reow."

Shoot. That definitely sounded like a kitten's version of "can confirm."

The volume was significantly lower than the original Pyewacket, but I'm nearly certain that kitten just agreed with my smug boyfriend.

CHAPTER 21

ERICK AND HIS NEW FURRY BEST FRIEND head into the apartment. Begrudgingly following the blissful pair, my appetite makes itself known by way of an audible abdominal grumble.

Sheriff Harper turns, and his kitty-cat pal rotates its ears toward me. Erick grins. "Diner?"

"Fine. I'm still not happy about whatever's going on with you two, but apparently I'm hungry."

He grins and places the tan bundle of fluff in the middle of the thick, winter-weight down comforter.

The tiny ball of fur disappears into the puffy depths. Despite my desire to have a pout, kittens really are the cutest things ever. I stifle a giggle and run into the closet to change out of my tear-soaked sweater.

The first T-shirt I grab is an absolute winner. A picture of a sleeping kitten above the phrase: "Please Don't Make Me Do Stuff."

When I exit the fashion command post that is my closet, Erick and Cutie-Pye are deep in a belly rub session.

I roll my eyes and exhale dramatically. Erick turns and hands me my jacket and a plain grey knit scarf. "Hey, I'll have your Harry Potter scarf cleaned. It was a total disaster after the original Pyewacket dragged it through the fields between the Barnes estate and the station."

The mention of Mr. Cuddlekins' previous incarnation brings a new pang of loss. Will this new kitten be so willing to sacrifice its lives for me? Silas seems to think everything will be all right, but I'm not sure his reincarnation theory is all it's cracked up to be.

A frosty wind blasts across the brooding great lake behind my bookshop and hits me in the face when I step onto the sidewalk. The chill seems to lift an invisible veil and instantly clarify my thoughts. "Erick, what did you do with Janet? She's obviously the suspect! She had plenty of time to poke around the mansion and steal that scarf. Did you charge her?"

His shoulders droop, and he shakes his head. "What's the old saying? A day late and a dollar short?" He clicks his tongue. "Initially, her alibi checked out. The clerk at the front desk remembered seeing Janet returning to the hotel, so we released her."

"She could've snuck back out, right?"

Erick nods halfheartedly. "Possibly. Or the clerk may have confused the days. Anyway, as soon as Paulsen got the statements from Dottie and Clyde, and clarified the timeline, she sent deputies to bring Janet back in. No joy. She's in the wind."

"I can grab my pendulum and find her in a jiffy." Spinning on my heel, I turn back to the bookstore.

"Hold on. That's not the worst part. When Deputy Johnson processed the paperwork last night, to put out the BOLO, he discovered Janet Ferro was only seven years old."

"What? Janet Ferro is clearly in her forties. What are you saying?"

Erick holds the door for me, and we step into Myrtle's Diner, pausing the conversation.

Odell offers his spatula salute, and I respond with a distracted wave.

We slide into a booth, accept our coffee with a quick thanks, and Erick continues. "What I'm saying is Janet Ferro is not her real name. Seven years ago, she paid a great deal of money to create a false identity. Complete with bank accounts, forged work histories, and even a manufactured genealogy. That was about twelve months, to the day, before she began working for Chiffon Cheryl's celebrity pastry chef empire. She clawed her way up the ranks and became Cheryl's personal assistant less than a year ago."

This job history nonsense is boring the bejeezus out of me. "Yaaaaawn. What is her actual name? Why did she go to all this trouble?"

"Her name is Maisy Deacon."

As the sounds fill the air, a story replays in my inner movie theater. "No way!"

Erick leans back and scrunches up his face. "I wouldn't make it up. Why?"

"That's crazy! That's the girl that Chiffon Cheryl, or just Cheryl at the time, got kicked out of culinary school. Maisy's cake was the one she stole that got her the name Chiffon Cheryl. Are you telling me that this woman held a grudge for decades and then spent her life savings on a revenge plot?"

He widens his eyes and shakes his head. "I guess I am. Hatred eats away at people from the inside. It's never good, but this is about as bad as it gets." Erick takes a sip of his coffee and slowly swallows. "I've got deputies all over the county searching, and she shouldn't be able to use any form of public transportation with that BOLO out."

"What about the driver?"

"What driver?"

"Her and Cheryl—they hired a driver to take them everywhere while they were in town. Have you checked with him?"

Erick shakes his head and grabs his cell phone. "Baird, put me through to Paulsen."

Our breakfast arrives. I ignore Erick's phone call and turn to Odell. Gripping his hand, I gesture for him to lean closer so I can update him with the condensed summary of last evening's séance disaster.

He looks at his watch and nods once. "As soon as the breakfast rush is over, I'll go see your grand-mother. Shame about her dress—and her shoe. I'll bet she's mad as a hornet."

"Believe it or not, I think she was actually more upset about Pyewacket. For once in her life, some-thing eclipsed couture."

We both chuckle, and he squeezes my shoulder. "Glad you're okay, kid."

"Me too, Gramps."

He grins, raps his knuckles twice on the table, and returns to the kitchen. Sheriff Harper ends his call and digs into his pancakes.

I open my mouth and wiggle my hands. "Well? What's the deal?"

"It's not really breakfast conversation. Can we finish our meal and talk about it in my office?"

The hairs on the back of my neck tingle, but I mind my psychic manners and close myself off from additional messages. "Copy that."

As you well know, it only takes me about five minutes or less to eat my breakfast. Erick is equally skilled with a fork, and once we gulp down the last of our go-go juice, we're on our way to the sheriff's station.

He holds the door for me, and when I step in, Deputy Baird's eyes widen. She taps madly on her phone—likely pausing her game of Furious Monkeys—and stashes it before the sheriff enters. I wink and lead the way to his office. Paulsen eases up from her desk chair and follows behind.

I'd love to close the door and leave her standing in the hallway, but every day I spend in Pin Cherry Harbor helps me learn a bit more about how manners make a person nice to know.

Instead, I take a seat, cross my arms over my chest, and wait for her to pull her gun on me.

Erick glances at the report on his desk. "Is this it?" He picks it up and flaps it twice.

"10-4. Gilbert took a statement from the passerby who found the car, and Johnson confirmed the ID of the victims with the medical examiner."

The sheriff shakes his head. "Thanks, Deputy.

Can you see to the press release and make sure Cheryl's body is transferred to the mortuary in Chicago?"

"10-4." The portly Deputy Paulsen turns on her squeaky-heeled work boots and stomps back to the bullpen.

"Sounds like the case is closed, Sheriff. But did you say *victims*? Plural? Care to share?"

He exhales. "A good Samaritan driver called this morning and reported the accident. You were absolutely right about Janet tricking that hired driver into taking her out of town."

"Tricking or forcing?" I tilt my head and scrunch up my face.

"Probably a little of both. The report mentions a firearm found at the crash site. Unfortunately for both of them, they didn't make it too far. According to the details, they were traveling at high speed when the hailstorm hit. As the vehicle crossed an elevated bridge, they hit a nasty patch of ice and flew over the guardrail. There were no survivors."

My throat tightens, and I shake my head in horror. "How awful for that poor man. Did he have any family?"

"Not according to the report. He was a drifter, working for cash under the table. Paulsen plans to have a conversation with the employer. Clearly, that's in violation of several legal hiring practices."

"Sure." My eyes glaze over as I imagine that nervous young Maisy at culinary school. Bursting with talent. Needing a little encouragement. A success or two. How awful. Three lives lost because a mean girl couldn't control her ego and ended up making a lifelong enemy.

"Moon? Earth to Moon?" Looking up to see Erick's face inches from mine shocks me from my reverie. His woodsy-citrus scent envelops me as he pulls me to my feet and holds me close. "You've been through a lot in the last twenty-four hours, Mitzy. This case is well and truly closed. Head home. Get some rest. I'll stop by the end of the day."

"What about Mrs. Charles and Clyde? You released them, right?"

"They were never under arrest, or even detained. I had a private word with Mrs. Charles. She's agreed to place Clyde in counseling. He needs some input about adult decisions from someone other than his mother."

The unspoken possibilities of the garden shed hang between us. No part of me believes Clyde would've followed through on his confused plan to protect his mother, but even a psychic gets it wrong sometimes. Score one for the timing of Mrs. Charles.

"Moon? Did you catch that? Paulsen took their

statements, and they returned to the estate. Why did you ask if they'd been released?"

"Oh, right. Sorry. I was— Will I be allowed to open the haunted house for Halloween? I know it's a weird question, but it's a fundraising event for a couple of worthwhile charities, and, after what happened—or almost happened—to Pyewacket, I want to double my efforts to raise money for the animal shelter and the pet cemetery. Can you give me the thumbs up?"

He smiles warmly and tucks a strand of hair behind my ear. "If you were anyone else—"

"But I'm not. I'm—" My breath stops short and my eyes widen. The memory of the question he asked that put the wheels of the séance disaster in motion floods to the forefront.

He doesn't need special abilities to know what I'm thinking. "I know your mother didn't have a chance to answer. And I'm incredibly sorry for throwing a monkey wrench into everything, but—"

I press a finger to his lips and shake my head. "Let's put a pin in it. This is not the energy either of us wants surrounding that question. I still have a parent on this side of the veil, if you need permission. So let's regroup. Deal?"

He swallows his emotion and forces a smile to the lips pinned beneath my finger. I press more firmly and wink. His lips part, and he gives my finger a playful bite.

Electricity shoots up and down my spine as I yank my finger from his mouth and wipe it against my T-shirt.

Seemingly for the first time, he notices the hilarious message emblazoned on my shirt. Erick bites his bottom lip and nods. "Appropriate."

I grin. "Thanks for breakfast, Sheriff. I'm gonna head back and see if I can make friends with Cutie-Pye—his temporary nickname—and I'll make all the arrangements to get my Halloween attraction back on track." My hopeful voice goes up at the end of my request, and he grins in defeat.

"Go ahead and open it." He steps away and reaches into his top desk drawer. Pushing aside protein bars, sticks of gum, and half a stale doughnut, he retrieves an object and extends his hand toward me.

"If it's the other half of that doughnut, I'm not interested."

Laughter reddens his cheeks as he flips his palm over to reveal the motion activation device for the prop coffin. "I'm sure Clyde knows where the plastic skeleton is. He can help you get everything set up, and I'll call the radio station to tell them to make an announcement."

"All right. Thanks. Tell them not to mention

any details about the murder, but to focus heavily on the cursed mansion angle."

He leans back and shakes his head.

I raise my hands in a pleading gesture. "It's for charity."

CHAPTER 22

DAMAGE FROM THE BRUTAL HAILSTORM is evident everywhere. Tree limbs are down, windows are broken, and cars dented. Clarence called to say he towed the Jeep to his shop. All the glass on my vehicle survived the frozen onslaught intact, but the roof and hood look like the surface of a golf ball. Fortunately, he loves preserving things and promised to locate her a new hood. I'm not worried about the roof. We'll call it character.

As I approach the imposing manor, the Latin motto twisted in iron above the gate catches my eye. Silas once told me it translated to "Divide and Conquer." I can assure you the Barnes family was nothing if not divided.

Now that the former head of staff for the Barnes family, Mrs. Charles, manages the estate, the grounds and impressive home are used exclusively for charitable events. I'm glad they cleared her and Clyde of any involvement with the murder, but if I'm honest, I'm still a little uneasy about seeing him today.

Before the incident in the garden, I never saw him as a threat. Now I have a twinge in my tummy. I don't like it.

Oh well, time to put on my big girl pants and make sure this attraction is ready to receive eager guests. The better the experience, the bigger the donations.

I hurry across the path. As I approach, Clyde steps out, clad in his usual uniform. Clean. Pressed. Nonthreatening.

"Good morning, Clyde. I got the green light from Sheriff Harper. Are you available to help me get everything set up for our guests?"

His eyes remain firmly downcast. He slips one hand from behind his back and rifles through the inner pocket of his suit jacket. Eventually, he extracts an envelope and passes it to me.

"Should I open this now, or is it a donation?"

His voice barely reaches the level of a whisper. "Now, please, Miss Moon."

"No problem." Flipping it over, I slide my finger under the flap and extract the folded pages within. Yes, *pages*. Four of them. The script is meticulous, and not a single cursive stroke is out of place. It only takes a quick scan of the first paragraph to figure out the purpose of the missive.

Dear Miss Moon,

I am very sorry about putting you to sleep in the garden and tying you up in the garden shed . . .

I'll spare you the details of his remorse, and, trust me, there are many.

As I skim through the pages, Clyde's repentance repeats itself multiple times. When I reach the last page, I reverently refold the letter and return it to the envelope. "Thank you, Clyde. It takes a very mature person to admit when they're wrong and apologize. I absolutely forgive you. I know what it's like to want to protect your mother. While I don't exactly condone your actions, I do understand. I promise you. Now, can you look at me and accept the forgiveness I'm offering you?"

His hands fidget behind his back; he licks his lips and swallows hard. "Yes, Miss Moon."

"Clyde, I need you to look at me." Pausing, I wait for his chin to rise a fraction of an inch and his dark eyes to meet mine. "I need you to promise me you'll never do that again. If you're ever in trouble, or Mrs. Charles is in trouble, you can ask for help. You don't have to take care of everything on your own. Someone once told me that there are people in this town who care about me and are willing to go out of their way to support me. I want to tell you the same thing. I'm here for you. Can you actually look at me, and promise to ask before you kidnap?"

I've never seen Clyde laugh, but the broad smile pushing his cheeks upward is the closest I'm likely to come.

His eyes dart up, and he nods. "Thank you, Miss Moon. I will ask next time."

Leave it to Clyde to take me precisely at my word. It's hardly my place to lecture him about making sure there isn't a next time. I think he got my point. "Great. Now let's put all that behind us and make this haunted house the best it can be."

Extracting the motion sensor from my pocket, I offer it to him. "Do you know how to replace this and fix the coffin?"

He nods and gently takes the device from my palm. "Yes, Miss Moon. My— Mrs. Charles tells me I have a gift for putting things back exactly as I found them. I've always been able to make mental pictures of the places I go, and draw them just like I was there."

"That's fascinating, Clyde. I'd love to see some of your drawings sometime."

His large chin finally lifts to level, and a smile touches his eyes. "You would?"

Reaching up to place a hand on his shoulder, I give it a squeeze. "Yes. I'm your friend, Clyde. That's what friends do."

He blinks nervously and his gaze returns to the ground. "I've never had a friend."

My heart breaks for him. Mrs. Charles did the best she could to raise him on her own after her abusive husband passed. She must've felt that sheltering him was the safest path forward. I wonder? How would I know? I have zero experience being a mother.

Unless you count Pyewacket, and I'd say recent events don't reflect too well on my child-rearing skills.

Clyde closes the front door behind us and leads the way through the attractions.

When we step through the French doors into the garden, my heart stutters and my mouth goes dry. I meant what I said to Clyde, about forgiving him and being his friend, but returning to the scene of the crime has its downside.

Thankfully, Mrs. Charles steps onto the patio a moment later with a plate full of fudgy-chocolate brownies decorated with green buttercream frosting vines and pumpkin candies. "I thought you two could use a little treat to fortify yourselves before you put the finishing touches on everything."

This is the nicest I've ever seen Mrs. Charles treat anyone on the planet. I'm definitely going to bask in this moment before it vanishes. "Thank you. Those look amazing! Is it all right to eat them out here, or should we come into the kitchen?"

"Pshaw. You go right ahead and eat them out here. I poured you each a mug of cocoa as well."

"Thank you." Part of me wonders if it's leftover cocoa from the other night's interrupted snicker-doodle debrief, but the rest of me doesn't care. Brownies and hot chocolate. Mrs. Charles is speaking my language.

She places the tray on the thick granite banister bordering the patio and retreats into the house.

Clyde picks up the plate of brownies and offers it to me. "Ladies first, Miss Moon."

"That's very kind. Thank you, Clyde." I pick up a large brownie and smile. In my heart of hearts, I know there's someone out there for him. Some patient, loving person who will appreciate all of Clyde's positive qualities. Sure, he's different. Aren't we all? Who among us is truly normal?

After downing our sustenance, the sugar rush powers us for several hours of resetting props and arranging decorations. Clyde and I even carve some fresh pumpkins to replace those damaged by hail.

Once we finish, he turns on all the outdoor lighting and the fog machine. I have to smile. "Everything looks amazing! You've got a real eye for this."

He shakes his head. "I only put things back the way they were. My mother was the one who followed your instructions, and I think she said, 'deciphered your chicken scratch.'"

Clyde's honesty pulls a belly laugh from me with ease. "I meant to tell you how lovely your handwriting is. That thoughtful letter you wrote was as beautiful as it was heartfelt."

"Thank you, Miss Moon."

We collect the last bits of packaging and loose paper, and Clyde turns off the displays.

"What time should I expect guests, Miss Moon?"

"Erick and I are hoping to arrive ahead of everyone. That should be about 5:00. I expect Artie to drop off the first busload of actual guests by 6:30. Will that work?"

He smiles broadly and nods. "I'll be ready, Miss Moon. I'll make sure everything is perfect."

"I know you will. See you in a few hours!"

He smiles and offers a casual wave. The only casual gesture I've ever witnessed from Clyde. It warms my heart and keeps a smile on my face all the way back to Pin Cherry proper.

CHAPTER 23

As the hand-carved population sign, with its thick white letters and faded pin cherries, whizzes past, Bless Choux comes to mind. I'd better stop at the bakery and bring Anne up to speed on the closure of this strange murder case.

Turning a couple of blocks before Main Street, I park on Third Avenue and hurry into the patisserie before the frigid air bites too deeply into my cheeks.

I barely have a foot through the door when Anne calls out. "Mitzy! Oh, Mitzy, I was hoping you'd stop in. Grab the table by the bric-à-brac, and I'll bring you your usual."

Nodding, I scan the store and, after careful consideration, assume that the "bric-à-brac" must be the tchotchkes—a wall of souvenirs. Mugs, T-shirts, aprons; you get the idea. Foster family number five opened up my vocabulary to a fair bit of Yiddish. Turned out I had a knack for the pronunciation. Who knew?

I take a seat at the table, and a moment later, Anne joins me. Her cheeks are flushed with excitement. They're almost as red as the pin cherries in—

"Um, Anne. These look like chocolate chip and pin cherry scones! Are you officially taking back your recipe?"

"I am! You're not going to believe what happened this morning!"

Looks like my news will have to wait. "Please, fill me in."

"My niece in Chicago sent me a text first thing this morning. Of course, I was up. You know the life of a baker."

To be clear, I know little to nothing about the life of a baker, but I'm not about to interrupt her flow, so I nod for her to continue.

"She said that the front-page story of the Tribune was all about Chiffon Cheryl! The article revealed all her fraudulent practices. It listed every recipe she'd ever stolen, whom she'd stolen it from, and approximately how much money she'd made from each theft. My niece said the article tanked her entire empire. In fact, details of the hoax she pulled on the baking community were so numerous, they didn't even mention her death until the continuation of the story on page eleven!"

My mouth hangs open like a busted suitcase at LaGuardia. "Wow. That's unbelievable."

Anne slaps her hand on the table and shakes her head. "I couldn't believe it. As soon as she told me, I started making a batch of my scones. Anyway, I was hoping Janet was still in town. I thought I'd invite her over so she could sample what they're actually supposed to taste like." She laughs and shrugs her shoulders blissfully.

"So, I guess you haven't heard?"

She places her elbows on the table and leans forward. "You mean there's even more good news?"

My face falls, and Anne shakes her head. "Uh oh, your face says not good news. What did I miss?"

Taking a deep breath, I unravel the details. "Did you hear about the accident on the bridge?"

She nods. "I think I overheard someone talking about it. Anyone we know?"

"More than you think. Janet was attempting to make a getaway. She forced her driver to take her out of town. There was ice. They went through the guardrail."

Anne covers her mouth with a hand and shakes her head as she blinks back tears. "I had no idea it . . . I promise you, I wasn't celebrating—"

"Oh, I know. It's not in your nature to be cruel. Thing is, that wasn't Janet who died in the crash."

"But you just said—"

"She'd assumed a false identity. Janet Ferro was actually Maisy Deacon."

You could have knocked Anne over with a feather. "How? I didn't even recognize her. Her hair . . . And her nose was . . . She never had glasses."

"She spent her life savings setting up the fake persona. I wouldn't be at all surprised to learn that she'd had a little plastic surgery and possibly colored her hair."

Anne continues to press a hand to her mouth and shake her head. "Poor Maisy." She looks down at the plate of scones and frowns. "Well, now I feel absolutely terrible about making scones."

My hand shoots across the table, and I pat her flour-covered fist. "Don't. You have every right to make your recipes in your bakery. And if anyone asks, you can tell them you baked them up as a memorial to your good friend Maisy Deacon."

Anne wipes under her eyes with the corner of her apron and nods. "That's true. That's what I'll say. I'm so sorry she wasn't able to find a better solution. How long did she work for Cheryl?"

"At least five years. She spent all that time gathering evidence and planning her revenge. Seems like the hub of all the action was Chicago, though. It's strange that she chose Pin Cherry Harbor for her last stand."

The friendly baker leans back in her chair and folds her hands in her lap. "Not really. I didn't tell you the whole story about culinary school."

"Do you want to tell me now?"

She sniffles and nods. "After Cheryl pulled that dirty trick on Maisy, I reported her. Unfortunately, Cheryl had already gained culinary darling status. The entire rest of the class supported her version of events, and I looked like a jealous student-baker suffering from a severe case of sour grapes. They suspended me, and I never went back."

My extrasensory perceptions tingle, and the mood ring on my left hand burns with a message. There's no need to look down. "Is there a bit more to the story?"

Anne exhales loudly and her arms flop to her sides. "Okay. Okay. I went back once. It was about three months later, after I'd tried to get into a couple of other culinary schools and been summarily denied. I was sure Cheryl had forced the CIA to blacklist me. So I snuck back in and smashed up a trophy case. I defaced her picture and stole one of the awards." She places an arm on the table and drops her forehead onto it, overcome with shame.

"You're a vandal? And you're not just rocking

the mic. You're a straight-up hoodlum!" My easy laughter breaks the tension, and Anne lifts her head.

"Oh, Mitzy. You don't know how many times I've relived that horrible night. Half of me is grateful there was no such thing as social media, and the other half of me is ashamed beyond belief. When I heard Cheryl had been murdered, I assumed the sheriff would arrest me in ten minutes. Anyone who went to that school knew I had a motive. Plus, I'd already shown a tendency toward violent retribution."

Reaching my hand across the table, I offer her a scone. "Let's let bygones be bygones, all right? You've more than made up for your youthful exuberance. And if there's anyone who knows how important it is to get a second chance, it's me. In case you've forgotten, they arrested me on suspicion of murdering my own grandfather when I first came to town."

Her eyes widen, and she guffaws despite her previous gloom. "I actually had forgotten. My goodness! That seems like a lifetime ago."

Anne's forthright nature brings a smile to my face. "Two or three lifetimes for me. I'm grateful that people like you, Doc Ledo, and Odell didn't judge me by those initial unfortunate events. I'd like to offer you the same absolution. Whatever happened, I'm sure you've paid for it in one way or another. Now you have this beautiful bakery, and" —I push the plate of scones an inch closer to her— "you have your recipe back!"

She shrugs her shoulders and eventually nods.

"I have to get back to the bookshop and get my costume organized for tonight. But promise me you're not going to beat yourself up about this. Maisy chose her path. I'm sure there were many times throughout the last five or six years that she could've abandoned her revenge plot. She didn't. She wasted her entire life trying to get even. Please, promise me you won't give this another moment's thought."

Anne finally picks up a scone and smiles. "I promise. What did you say? Bygones? Consider it gone."

Selecting a scone from the dish, I lift mine and bump it against hers in a pastry toast. "Bygones."

CHAPTER 24

THE CROOKED SIGN taped in the window at the Bell, Book & Candle tells me Twiggy is still on her book collection trip. Letting myself in, I climb over the chain at the bottom of the wrought-iron circular staircase and stop when I reach the loft.

The carpets have all been replaced, and the oak reading tables are once again in neat rows. Each desk features a freshly polished brass reading lamp with a green-glass shade. Silas is a man of many talents.

When I step into the apartment, something stirs on my enormous four-poster bed.

"Pyewacket? It's you, right?"

"Re-oow." This vocalization reminds me of a tolerant greeting he once offered to Erick. That was back in the days before they became beastie and bestie!

He's really sticking it to me. I'm not sure why. He's the one who chose to sacrifice his remaining lives to save Grams. Yeesh! It's not like I threw him into the abyss.

Walking toward the bed, I'm only marginally surprised when the head that pops up from the depths of the down comforter is nearly twice the size of the kitten noggin I saw this morning.

"Well, well, well. It looks like we're going to be treated to a supernatural growth rate. Do you remember who I am now?"

"RE-ow." Feed me.

"Take it easy, son. This adolescent version of you needs to learn some respect for the girl with the opposable thumbs."

He squeezes his eyes closed dismissively.

"Fine. I suppose you expect me to get you some Fruity Puffs?"

Without warning, he leaps from the bed and bounds into the closet.

At least some things haven't changed.

Rushing in after him, I hope to sneak a peek at his secret exit. Dagnabbit! Too late. The furry fiend is gone, and he has once again outmaneuvered me.

When I reach the back room, he's eagerly

clawing at the cabinet that holds his favorite sugary children's cereal.

Now, this is the wildcat I remember. Fetching a bowl from the cupboard, I pour him a heaping helping of cereal.

He dives in, and I risk testing the reincarnation theory a bit more. I reach toward his back, but before my fingers get within scratching distance, he spins and thwacks my hand with a needle-clad paw.

"Ouch!"

Fresh beads of blood bubble to the surface along the row of warning scratches. It's my own fault. I can hardly be upset with Pye. I know the rules, and I chose to ignore them. This is fair punishment.

Also, they're not deep, and they've already stopped bleeding. I dab my hand with a paper towel, toss it in the trash, and head back upstairs to organize the costumes.

Erick was going to get changed at his own house, but I told him the zombie makeup had to be applied first, and I didn't think it would be a good idea to drive his police cruiser once I completed that task.

Folks in Pin Cherry might be used to a little nonsense on Mischief Night, but if they thought their beloved sheriff had been turned into a zombie, that might be a bridge too far.

Pyewacket returns, leaps to the top of the antique armoire beside the entrance, and performs his post-snack ablutions.

"What do you think, Cutie-Pye? Should I change out the dead roses for black roses? I feel like the dead roses make more of a statement. And black roses might not be all that visible in a darkened haunted house. Thoughts?"

An answer comes, but not from my furry friend.

"Oh, I think you have to stick with the dead roses, sweetie."

"Grams! How many times have we discussed this? Slow. Sparkly. Reentry." She giggles and swirls around me. "Honestly, Mitzy. You should be used to this by now. You live with a ghost. You should always assume I'll be popping in unexpectedly and be ready for it."

"Seriously, Grams? Instead of you taking the time to follow my one rule, you expect me to be in a constant state of readiness for your untimely pop-ins?" Placing a hand on my hip, I narrow my gaze and wait for her answer.

"Your one rule! Do you even listen to yourself? You have so many rules, I can't keep track. First it's the thought-dropping, then it's no heels, then—"

My cheeks flush. "All right. Point taken. I'll meet you halfway. You try to remember the proper reentry, and I'll try to be prepared when you don't."

She smirks and floats close enough to put her shimmering hand on my cheek. "Perfect, dear. The best relationships are built on compromise."

"Oh brother."

"Speaking of the best . . . What time will Erick be here? And do I get to do his hair?"

"He'll be here as soon as he can. He's the sheriff, and the safety of Birch County comes first. And you absolutely do not get to do his hair! I will attempt to convince him that slicking it back with his signature pomade is unnecessary. I feel an undead groom would be more unkempt. We'll see how that goes."

"Well, you let me know if you need backup, sweetie. I'm happy to get in there and give it a good old ghost muss about if necessary."

"Oh, I have no doubt, Grams." We share a chuckle. "I'll start my zombie makeup while I wait."

She nods as though it's an everyday conversation.

As I walk into the bathroom, I fire off a quick text to my beau. "Getting into makeup now. Will you be here soon?"

BING. BONG. BING.

Grams and I shout in unison, "He's here!"

PING.

Glancing at my phone as I hurry to the alleyway door, Erick's text reply makes me chuckle.

"Wow. It's almost like you're psychic or something."

Pushing open the door, I purse my lips and tilt my head. "Ha ha, Sheriff."

He scoops his arms around me and kisses me hungrily. "I had to get that out of my system before all this nonsense makeup gets slathered all over. Go easy on me, Moon. I can't stand that stuff. When we had to put camo cover on our faces, I seriously would've— Never mind. Definitely not a fan. Just take it easy on my skin, okay?"

"By all means, Your Majesty. I shall use the utmost care when I apply the ghoulish effects to your porcelain cheeks."

He rolls his eyes and tickles me mercilessly.

Squealing with delight, I run for the stairs and get all wadded up, trying to jump the chain.

Saving me from any serious harm, Erick gets me solidly on my feet. As he untangles the chain from the railing, my phone pings with yet another text.

It's from Twiggy, and I have to read it out loud. "Twiggy says, 'Hook it back up.'"

Erick secures the chain and looks at me in confusion.

I shrug. "How did she know? The alarm didn't even go off, and I know that wasn't thirty seconds."

He takes my hand, leads me up the stairs, and shrugs. "Maybe she has it set up to text her before

the alarm goes off. You know, since you always—"
He stops speaking suddenly, and his eyes widen.

"No, please finish that sentence. I would love to
hear what you're about to say, Sheriff."

He presses his thumb and forefinger together
and zips an imaginary zipper across his lips.

"Good man, Harper. That skill will serve you
well in our future."

Pulling me close, he whispers hotly in my left
ear. "I like it when you say things about our future."

CHAPTER 25

I NEVER IMAGINED PUTTING makeup on someone else. I barely bother to put it on myself!

The act of leaning extremely close to Erick Harper and creating zombie bruises, sunken eyes, and fake bloody wounds is more intimate than it sounds.

For one thing, I have to stare directly into his piercing blue eyes far too many times. And each time I lean in to apply another layer of shading, his minty breath raises goosebumps across my flesh.

It's a good thing I'm committed to hosting this fundraising event. Otherwise, there's a very good chance he would never make it out of my apartment!

Cooler heads prevail, and at long last, Erick and I are the perfect zombie wedding cake topper. He's a bedraggled, oozing groom, and I'm a rotting corpse bride.

Grams attempts to be delighted for us. "Oh, gosh, you two sure do make a pair."

"Thanks, Grams. I'm pretty sure the only thing two people can make is a pair. I'm sorry this isn't the wedding photo you'd hoped for."

"Mitzy, you're such a hoot!"

I wink and throw her a finger gun. "You're not wrong."

My decaying groom interrupts the banter. "Better hit the road, Mitzy. I know you want to arrive before the first busload."

"Right. Let's go."

As I wait for the bookcase to slide open, Erick calls out, "Do you want me to grab your bouquet?"

I can't explain it, but the question sends me into a fit of giggles. As I move to wipe the laughter-tears from my face, Grams explodes near my left ear. "No! Don't you dare mess that makeup. As much as I dislike it, I suppose it's better when it's perfect."

"There are tears running down my face."

She vanishes momentarily, and Erick gasps. From his perspective, a lone facial tissue bounces through the air in my apartment.

She hands it to me, and I carefully dab the moisture from my face.

"Now, the two of you better get going. I will expect a full report."

Squaring my shoulders, I pop a salute in her general direction. "10-4, Sergeant Grams."

She rolls her ethereal eyes and floats nose to nose. "Do you need me to vacate the premises this evening?" She points to her right eye and winks comically.

"Um, Erick? Will you be accompanying me back to the apartment this evening, or do you have other plans?"

He puts his arms straight out in front of him, Frankenstein's monster-style, and shambles toward me. His voice is monotone and robotic. "Zombie have no plans."

Rolling my eyes and giggling, I push his stiff arms away. "Seems like that's a yes, Grams. We would appreciate some privacy this evening."

She winks a second time and phases through the wall.

As we walk down to the first floor, I toss some stage directions over my shoulder. "By the way, you're not Frankenstein's monster. You're a flesh-eating zombie that loves brains and can't talk."

He shrugs and hooks the chain behind us. "You don't know. Modern-day zombies are quite advanced. They're faster, they can talk, and they work as a team."

Sliding my hand under his tattered tuxedo jacket, I whisper softly, "Oh, I'm all about team-work, Sheriff."

He grins and pushes open the alleyway door. "You're going to regret taunting me once that makeup comes off, Moon."

A thrill races across my skin as I climb into his Nova. He obviously took my advice about zombie sheriffs and swapped his patrol car for his "speed about town like a teenage maniac" car.

True to form, we arrive at the Barnes estate in record time.

The place looks amazing! Clyde and Mrs. Charles absolutely outdid themselves.

The eerie lighting, heavy layer of ground fog, and the cacophony of spooky sounds are a simply wonderful salute to All Hallows' Eve.

"This place looks fantastic, Moon. I bet you'll raise a ton of cash for the animal shelter. They're lucky to have you in their corner."

"And I'm lucky to have *you* in my corner, Sheriff Harper."

The door opens, and my breath catches in my throat. Clyde never mentioned he would be wearing a costume. He's dressed as Igor, the hunch-back sidekick of Dr. Frankenstein. "Clyde! You look fabulous. Did you come up with that costume yourself?"

He nods. "I hope it's all right, Miss Moon."

"It's more than all right. It's fantastic! The guests are going to love it." The costumed Clyde has me so distracted I nearly miss the giant Angel of Death.

The dark and mysterious celestial on the right side of the door flaps her massive electronic wings and leans toward us. "Names, please."

The voice modulator gives her tone a creepy echo. "Mitzy Moon and Erick Harper."

She glances briefly at her list, checks off our names with a quill pen made from a faux sharpened bone, and hands us a black feather. "You may enter."

I accept the feather and whisper, "You're doing a wonderful job. I want to remind you, this is a fundraiser. So, if someone isn't on the list, please offer them the opportunity to purchase a ticket. If push comes to shove, make a note of anyone who isn't able to pay, and the Duncan-Moon Foundation will cover their fees."

She reaches to her neck and turns off the voice modulator. Her sweet voice tingles in the crisp fall air. "You got it, Mitzy."

Erick chuckles. "I should get one of those voice modulators for interrogations. I bet I could get criminals to crack in record time with that ominous, booming echo."

Gripping his hand, I pull him into the hall of portraits. "I think you have a pretty good record as its stands, Harper."

Despite the rules about not smudging makeup, Erick kisses me in the light of vaporous ghosts and creepy portraits. "You outdid yourself, Moon. This place will be the talk of the town until Christmas!"

We pass into the next room, and Erick jumps when the door slams closed behind us.

"Easy, Sheriff. That's supposed to happen."

He chuckles nervously, and I squeeze his hand.

We hurry through the remaining rooms to complete one last check and head into the garden/Halloween cemetery to sample the treats Mrs. Charles prepared.

We're surprised to discover she's dressed as a nurse in a surgery gone wrong! "Mrs. Charles! Where did you get all that fake blood?"

She leans close with her giant plastic hypodermic needle. "*Fake?*"

Taking recent events into consideration, I'm unnerved by her response.

She pulls the oversized syringe back and chuckles. "I made a huge bucket today and drizzled some on the pumpkins by the entrance and a little more on a few of these Styrofoam gravestones. I hope you like it."

My voice sticks in my throat, but Erick saves the

day. "It looks great. Mind if I try some of these eye-ball cookies?"

She picks up a tray and offers them to us. "Please. These were such fun to make."

Erick and I take our places in the cemetery, where Clyde thoughtfully placed two chairs and an outdoor heater. He really did think of everything.

The rumble of the school bus engine and a loud squeal of its brakes alert us to the arrival of the first bus.

The Angel of Death's booming voice echoes through the night air and receives several screams and giggles.

"Looks like we're off to a good start, Sheriff."

He slips an arm around my waist. "I can promise you the ending will be even better."

Gulp.

The screams of laughter creep closer as the first group of guests passes through the various rooms in the mansion.

When they reach the patio, Mrs. Charles encourages them to explore the cemetery before they grab their treats.

The first couple to promenade past the motion activation device gets quite a scare. The girl screams and jumps into her date's arms.

Perfection.

The remaining guests grab their treats and exit through the side gate near us.

We lunge forward and claw the air, mumbling, "Brains. Brains."

They leave a stream of laughter and screams in their wake, as the patrons head to the pickup location.

The bus pulls up to drop off another load of passengers just as the first group exits.

I have to hand it to Artie. She's a pro.

One group melds into the next as the hours slip away. Thoughts of the senseless murder and the corpse we so recently found in our prop coffin are never far from my mind. However, the throngs of visitors passing through the attraction mean there will be plenty of working capital for the local no-kill animal shelter. That's my takeaway from all of this. Closing my eyes, I exhale, push the unfortunate revenge-based events from my mind, and focus on giving back to my community.

Sheriff Harper is briefly called into action when a small child goes missing in the haunted dining room.

With the help of my extra senses, we quickly find the young boy hiding under the enormous table. The thick cloth covering the tabletop reaches all the way to the floor and offered him an irresistible fort. He hadn't even realized his mother had left the room.

Hugs and thank yous all around.

Promptly at midnight, the attraction officially closes. We encourage all remaining guests to come into the cemetery and enjoy the last of the hand-made treats in the light of the full moon.

Whether the howl of the wolf is part of the soundtrack, or a real-life endorsement, shall remain a mystery.

Erick takes advantage of things winding down and smears my zombie makeup with his passionate kiss. "Next time I kiss you in a wedding dress, Moon, it's going to be for keeps."

If inspiring tingles could be converted into energy, I could power a major city for a week with that comment!

End of Book 20

A NOTE FROM TRIXIE

Whew! That was a close call for Pyewacket. I'll keep writing them if you keep reading . . .

The best part of "living" in Pin Cherry Harbor continues to be feedback from my early readers. Thank you to my alpha readers/cheerleaders, Angel and Michael. HUGE thanks to my fantastic beta readers who continue to give me extremely useful and honest feedback: Veronica McIntyre and Nadine Peterse-Vrijhof. And big "small town" hugs to the world's best ARC Team – Trixie's Mystery ARC Detectives!

My diligent editor Philip Newey continues to point out plot holes and challenge me as a writer. Thanks to him, I enjoy getting notes and polishing each story. I'd also like to give buckets of gratitude to Roxx at Proof Perfect for jumping in at the eleventh hour! Any remaining errors are my own.

Here's to passing on a little Halloween happiness to each of you!

FUN FACT: My very first costume—ever—was a witch.

My favorite line from this case: "My furry overlord is going to be insufferable if I make it out of this alive." ~Mitzy

I'm currently writing book twenty-one in the Mitzy Moon Mysteries series. Mitzy, Grams, and Pyewacket got into plenty of trouble in book one, *Fries and Alibis*. But I'd have to say that book three, *Wings and Broken Things*, is when most readers say the series becomes unputdownable.

I hope you'll continue to hang out with us.

Trixie Silvertale (September 2022)

Mitzy Moon Mysteries 2 1

**A puzzling fire. A pur-
loined keepsake. Can
our psychic sleuth un-
cover the connection
before it's ashes to
ashes?**

Mitzy Moon adores the
Winter Extravaganza. In
fact, she's so eager to sip
mulled cider this year, she's
volunteered to help with
set-up. But when a myste-
rious blaze destroys the curling arena, her holiday
treats could be the next thing to go up in flames.

With the whole town acting odd and visions of a snow princess dancing in her head, Mitzy risks her own safety to pursue the truth. She ignores ominous warnings from the sheriff, Ghost-ma and her entitled feline, and may have leaped out of the frying pan and into an inferno...

Can Mitzy's snooping reveal what history has hidden, or will this Yuletide be her last?

Vandals and Yule Scandals is the twenty-first book in the hilarious Mitzy Moon Mysteries paranormal cozy mystery series. If you like snarky heroines, supernatural intrigue, and a dash of romance, then you'll love Trixie Silvertale's Christmas caper.

Buy *Vandals and Yule Scandals* to pinch a pyro today!

Grab yours!
readerlinks.com/l/2720512

Scan this QR Code with the camera on your phone. You'll be taken right to the Mitzy Moon Mysteries series page. You can easily grab any mysteries you've missed!

Once you're in the Club, you'll also be the first to receive updates from Pin Cherry Harbor and access to giveaways, new release announcements, short stories, behind-the-scenes secrets, and much more!

Scan this QR Code with the camera on your phone. You'll be taken right to the page to join the Club!

THANK YOU!

Trying out a new book is always a risk and I'm thankful that you rolled the dice with Mitzy Moon. If you loved the book, the sweetest thing you can do (*even sweeter than pin cherry pie à la mode*) is to leave a review so that other readers will take a chance on Mitzy and the gang.

Don't feel you have to write a book report. A brief comment like, "Can't wait to read the next book in this series!" will help potential readers make their choice.

★★★★★
Leave a quick review HERE
https://readerlinks.com/l/2471218
★★★★★

Thank you kindly, and I'll see you in Pin Cherry Harbor!

Heists and Poltergeists: Paranormal Cozy Mystery

Blades and Bridesmaids: Paranormal Cozy Mystery

Scones and Tombstones: Paranormal Cozy Mystery

Vandals and Yule Scandals: Paranormal Cozy Mystery

More to come!

MAGICAL RENAISSANCE FAIRE MYSTERIES

Explore the world of Coriander the Conjurer. A fortune-telling fairy with a heart of gold!

Book 1: ***All Swell That Ends Spell*** – A dubious festival. A fatal swim. Can this fortune-telling fairy herald the true killer?

Book 2: ***Fairy Wives of Windsor*** – A jolly Faire. A shocking murder. Can this furtive fairy outsmart the killer?

Join Sydney Coleman and her unruly ghosts, as they solve mysteries in a truly haunted mansion!

Book 1: ***Moonlight and Mischief*** – She's desperate for a fresh start, but is a mansion on sale too good to be true?

Book 2: ***Moonlight and Magic*** – A haunted Halloween tour seem like the perfect plan, until there's murder...

Book 3: ***Moonlight and Mayhem*** – An unwelcome visitor. A surprising past. Will her fire sale end in smoke?

ABOUT THE AUTHOR

USA TODAY Bestselling author Trixie Silvertale grew up reading an endless supply of Lilian Jackson Braun, Hardy Boys, and Nancy Drew novels. She loves the amateur sleuths in cozy mysteries and obsesses about all things paranormal. Those two passions unite in her Mitzy Moon Mysteries, and she's thrilled to write them and share them with you.

When she's not consumed by writing, she bakes to fuel her creative engine and pulls weeds in her herb garden to clear her head (*and sometimes she pulls out her hair, but mostly weeds*).

Greetings are welcome:
trixie@trixiesilvertale.com

Made in United States
North Haven, CT
10 March 2023

33781696R00157